THE LEGEND OF ONIONHEAD

By

Gregory Scott

The legend of "Onionhead" appears in many sources around the world. This legend has an international reach, and not just as a tale about a man, but about a community overcome by superstition and blind fear. Consistently, articles in other countries specify Slidell as the source of this legend. There are minor variances in articles from country to country. Yet, almost all agree that these events occurred in Slidell, Louisiana, USA. This book is based on that legend.

About the Author

Gregory "Greg" Scott is a historian, storyteller, and lifelong seeker of the forgotten. Born in New Orleans in 1960 and raised across the United States as the son of a U.S. Army soldier, Greg developed an early fascination with the places others pass through—the small towns, rural outposts, and overlooked corners where local legend and personal memory intertwine.

His own path has been as varied as the stories he tells. An honorably discharged veteran of the U.S. Army's 2nd Squadron, 9th Cavalry Regiment (Air Mobile/Air Assault; Rapid Deployment Force), Greg went on to serve in law enforcement and engineering & construction consulting before turning to his current calling: researching and preserving the stories of the past. Since becoming Director and Curator of the Slidell Museum in 2019, he has helped reconstruct the historical record of the town following the devastation of Hurricane Katrina—piece by piece, story by story.

The Legend of Onionhead was born not from local rumor but from global discovery. While researching an unrelated topic in South America, Greg stumbled upon a haunting, recurring legend, a disfigured young man, misunderstood and unjustly killed, who lived on through local folklore. This story, translated and adapted across borders, began appearing in source material from Southeast Asia, Eastern Europe, and North Africa. In every version, the origin traced back to one place: Slidell, Louisiana. And in every version, the details remained over 90% the same.

Struck by this haunting consistency, Greg saw the need not just to retell the legend, but to give it narrative weight—to craft something with the emotional resonance of The Legend of Sleepy Hollow or The Tell-Tale Heart. With careful reverence for folklore and an eye for historical texture, he created a fictional tale based on a global ghost story, rooted deeply in the soul of a Southern Louisiana town.

Greg holds several degrees, including History, English, Philosophy, and Public History, and is a member of numerous academic and civic organizations, including the Lions Club and several collegiate honor societies. He is also the author of local history anthologies and technical publications.

Through his work, Greg bridges memory and myth, always seeking the deeper truth behind the stories we inherit—and the ones we pass down.

Introduction

This book began as a whisper.

While researching an unrelated topic in South America, I stumbled upon a strange, persistent tale—a young man, disfigured and misunderstood, who was wrongly accused and killed by his neighbors. A haunting. A legend. I brushed it off at first. Then I found it again. And again.

In Southeast Asia. In Eastern Europe. In forgotten corners of translation archives. And always, inexplicably, the story pointed back to one place: Slidell, Louisiana. A town I now call home. A place I thought I understood.

Nearly every version shared the same bones—thirteen pieces, a porcelain doll, a storm, a cemetery. The details were chillingly consistent, yet always hollow. The legend existed, yes—but without depth, without character, without the grief and the guilt and the lives behind it.

And so, I set out to give this legend flesh. To tell not just a ghost story, but a human one. A story of fear and injustice, of sorrow and silence, of love that couldn't save and hate that couldn't be buried. A story that might have happened anywhere—but according to history, happened here.

This is a work of fiction. But like all folklore, it may still hold a truth that facts alone can't capture.

This is The Legend of Onionhead.

I hope it lingers.

— G.D. Scott

Table of Contents

PROLOGUE

The dogs were getting closer.

The distinctive form of Solomon Moreau slipped deeper into the swamp, the mud pulling at his ankles like gripping hands. His chest heaved. His feet bled. The shouts behind him grew louder—men's voices, rough and panicked, thick with liquor and vengeance.

"Fan out!"

"He's this way!"

"God help us if he slips away again!"

They weren't looking for justice.

They were looking for someone to punish.

And Solomon, with his disfigured skull and twisted features, his one wandering eye, and a jaw that didn't sit quite right, with his silence and strange ways, had always been easy to blame.

The swamp, at least, knew him.

The cypress trees bent like protective old women over his path. He slid beneath a curtain of Spanish moss and vanished into black water up to his waist. Somewhere behind him, a dog barked—short and sharp—followed by a splash and shouted curses as one of his pursuers lost their footing.

Solomon pressed forward, breath shallow, heart hammering like a snared bird.

He could still see her face.

The little girl.

Mary-Ellen.

1

He didn't kill her. Never touched her. But that didn't matter.

When folks found a child murdered, and a man like him living in the nearby wooded swamp with his deformities and lonesome ways, it didn't take more than a whisper to turn mourning into rage.

He ducked beneath a leaning trunk, scraping his shoulder on the bark. A cottonmouth slithered away from his path, unbothered by his presence. The swamp didn't flinch at Solomon. It knew he belonged. Always had.

But the men—they were invaders.

He could smell the burning kerosene from the torches they carried. He could hear the crunch and squish of sticks and mud as they fought through the undergrowth and mud.

They weren't just chasing him.

They meant much more if they caught up to him.

They meant to make sure he never came out of the swamp again.

Then—

A gunshot cracked the air.

The bullet struck a tree inches from his head, spraying bark into his hair.

"Solomon Moreau!" bellowed Gervais Boudreaux. "We know it was you! You ain't foolin' no one no more! Show yourself, you monster!"

The others whooped and hollered, emboldened.

Solomon didn't stop.

He turned toward the deeper, boggier part of the swamp—where the ground sank and the mist rolled in thick as cream. Where no man but him dared to go. Where his mother once whispered long ago: "When the world turns on you, baby, go where the world can't follow. The swamp got places no fire can burn."

Another shot. Another bullet.

But Solomon was already gone—vanished into a wall of cattails and black vines.

Behind him, the flames of the torches bobbed like angry stars.

Ahead of him, the fog opened like a veil.

And somewhere—somewhere deeper—a woman's voice seemed to hum.

###

1. THE CALM BEFORE THE STORM

It's a hot morning in the summer of 1925, and the small town stirs with the slow rhythm of rural life. Dirt roads worn smooth by generations lead to a stone well that stands in front of the Slidell Town Hall, where people come and go in a steady trickle with galvanized pails swinging and clanking gently in their hands.

Women in faded cotton dresses and broad-brimmed hats walk with quiet purpose, their shoes kicking up little puffs of dust. Some still have their aprons tied around their waists, evidence of bread making or laundry that was half-finished at home. Smaller children skip along beside them, bare feet toughened by the dirt roads, eager for a reason to delay chores. Older children carry buckets of their own to gather water for their family.

People along the way sit on porches sipping drinks and fanning themselves, even at this early hour. People stop and chat, exchange news, recipes, and gossip. News often traveled faster this way than through the newspaper.

All day, men would come home early from the fields or head to them, pausing near the well to roll up their sleeves, their shirts damp with sweat. They tip their hats to passersby, exchange quick words—news of a new calf, the threat of rain, or Mrs. Haverly's peach preserves.

The well is a gathering place, half utility and half ritual. Neighbors nod and smile as they wait their turn, chatting about the schoolteacher's new boarder, or the new Model-T that someone's cousin bought in the next town over. Water sloshes in buckets and tin dippers clink against the well's stone rim. A breeze stirs the dust and brings with it the scent of wildflowers and wood smoke.

This is a place where time moves slowly, where people know each other's names and stories, and the walk to the well is as much a social call as it is a necessity.

#

By mid-June, Slidell sweated beneath a thick grey sky that never quite broke open. The air clung to the skin like syrup, and bayous had begun to swell just a bit higher than usual, licking hungrily at the muddy banks. Cypress trees stood like silent watchers, cloaked in curtains of moss, and even the birds seemed quieter, as if not having the energy to sing.

It was a season of stillness.

A few times a day, trains would rattle through town with a clang and a clatter, dragging heat and dust in their wake. People would pause in their errands just long enough to watch it pass—habit, not curiosity. The railroad had once given the town life, but now seemed to simply pass through it.

Often, children played barefoot in the churchyard, where weeds curled around the fence posts like green snakes. The bell in the steeple was seldom used, the preacher preferring to clap two wooden planks together. He said it gave a more *honest sound*.

Folks talked on porches and in the general store, fans creaking back and forth in lazy hands. They talked about the weather mostly, about crops, and about the man who had gone blind last winter—but still claimed he could see ghosts behind his eyelids.

The schoolhouse bell rang. The grocer swept her stoop. The doctor checked his pocket watch, like always. The preacher clapped his boards and warned of sin. On the surface, everything in the small town looked the same.

#

The Sun burned high over the tin-roof of the one-room schoolhouse. The bell rang out, and the children spilled into the yard, free from lessons and blackboard scoldings. Their laughter bounced like marbles down a dirt path that led to the main road.

At the far edge of the yard, where the woods crept close, a circle of children played a rope jumping game—jumping and chanting as the heavy hemp twisted in rhythm. Their voices rose and fell in sing-song unison, their shoes scuffing up dust with the rhythm of some deep and ancient beat.

Willy in the trees, don't look twice,

Blue like fire, but cold as ice.

Follow Willy, don't look back,

Willy walks the shadow's track.

Keep your feet and hold your breath,

One wrong step and you're with death.

If Willy finds you, don't you run—

Willy dances when you're done.

If you see him, close your eyes,

He don't like no alibis.

Willy walks where liars go—

He's the fire and you're the smoke.

The sing-song chant went on, over and over. The rope slapped the dirt, then whooshed through the air. A girl missed her step and tumbled out, giggling as she gave her place to another. Their faces were smudged with dirt and sun. Their eyes were alive with the harmless thrill of ghost stories told in daylight. The stories of *"Willy-the-Whisp,"* the glowing blue light in the swamp, were common knowledge to everyone in town. The old rumors and ghostly stories had been told for as long as anyone could recall. Nothing but superstition and imagination run wild.

Beneath it all, something had begun to stir.

The animals knew first. Dogs barked at nothing in the night. Chickens refused to roost. A calf was born with no eyes.

And the days dragged on, hot and breathless.

###

2. THE CABIN IN THE SWAMP

At the far edge of the town, where the land softens into dark water, and the cypress trees grow fat and twisted with moss, there was a trail leading off from the railroad tracks. A bit overgrown from lack of use, the weedy trail leads into the woods, past tall pines and other trees. Soon, the path begins to narrow, and the ground grows soggy. The pines and hardwood trees fade away, replaced by swampy undergrowth, cypress trees, and other wetland plants. At the end of the path stands the cabin of Marie Moreau and her son Solomon, a weather-grey structure, sagging with time and half-swallowed by vines and shadow.

It was built by Solomon's grandfather, or so Marie always said, long before state lines carved through the region. The foundation rests on low stone piers to keep it above the marsh's shifting moods. Built with cypress wood, now aged to silver, it groans under the weight of time and weather, standing sturdier than it appears—like Solomon.

The Moreau cabin in the swamp was spoken of in half-whispered tones. No one comes this deep unless they mean to. This far into the swamp, the path is narrow and winding, hemmed by cutting palmetto fronds, thorny vines, and black willows. Mosquitoes swarm thick as breath, and the croaking of frogs is nearly constant—so loud they sometimes sounded like voices.

To the people of Slidell, the cabin was a place of whispers and ghost stories, superstition and imaginations gone wild.

To Solomon, it is a sanctuary.

#

Inside, the cabin smells of dried sage, damp wood, and the faint sweetness of elderflower. There is no electricity. Light comes from homemade beeswax candles and oil lamps, which Solomon tends with patient hands. Their glow makes the shadows dance, flickering like spirits celebrating.

Every shelf is crowded with bundles of herbs in jars or hung upside down—boneset, bay laurel, yarrow, red clover. The jars are labeled in his mother's curling hand—feverfew, valerian, wild ginger, cramp bark. Some say Marie Moreau's tea could calm a fever better than any doctor's tonic. Others had far less regard for her 'witchery.'

There are two small rooms separated by a thin, threadbare curtain. His mother had a room in the back, and Solomon slept on a narrow cot in the front room. The cot was covered by a handmade quilt, sewn by Marie when he was small, stitched from faded dresses and old feed sacks. He keeps it neat and reverent. A wooden crucifix hangs above the cot, but it is flanked on one side by a bundle of dried rue, and on the other a little pouch of graveyard dirt tied with a red thread—all Christian and folk protections, the way his mother had taught him.

Solomon owns a mirror that he keeps covered with a black cloth.

He hasn't looked in it for years.

He avoids it not because he is ashamed, but because he fears that if he ever stares at it too long, he might begin to believe what people have said about him his entire life. Instead, he puts his faith in growing things. In the hush of trees. In the comfort of his mother's voice echoing through his memory: "You ain't a monster, bébé. You're just made of a different clay. And

9

different ain't never meant wicked—just sacred in another tongue."

A cast-iron stove heats the place in winter. Beside it, there is a chipped enamel basin for washing. A locked trunk in the corner holds their most sacred things: a photo of Marie as a young woman, her eyes proud and soft; a pressed flower she once tucked behind Sol's ear; a worn leather-bound notebook with recipes, treatments, and mixtures.

There are carvings on the floor—symbols Marie etched there with a bone-handled knife, for warding off illness and keeping the spirits still.

#

Solomon wakes with the birds. He walks the swamp and woods barefoot more often than not, silent and observant. He gathers plants, herbs, and other things for his mother, knowing which trees bleed healing sap, which mushrooms kill, and which plants sleep by day and bloom at night.

He spends hours helping to prepare bundles of carefully wrapped herbs bound in string or cloth. Bundles that are left on porches when someone is ill or pregnant, or grieving. No note. No name.

He listens to the frogs. He speaks to the wind. And sometimes, late at night, he sings old lullabies in a voice low and strange, part in French, a little in English, and part in something much older.

No one saw Marie or Solomon much, except on the few occasions when he came to town to fetch nails or some such things. Even then, Solomon never lingered. Children watched him like a stray dog might watch a snake—curious, but ready to flee. When he does go to town, he keeps his head down, body wrapped in a long coat no matter the heat. Some folks cross themselves. Others throw insults and taunts. But every now and then, a mother will leave a coin on her windowsill the morning after he's passed by, just in case the bundle she found was meant for her child.

3. WOMAN OF SHADOWS

Marie Moreau was a Creole medicine woman, born under a blood moon in the back room of a sugar plantation where her mother worked the boiling vats and her grandmother whispered prayers in *patois* so old it scraped the air like cane knives.

Marie was not a woman who asked permission. She gathered roots by the bayou, spoke to snakes like they were gossiping cousins, and knew the names of every leaf that could save you—or curse you. She lived her life under her own terms, which made a lot of townsfolk uneasy.

In Slidell, they called her *"femme des ombres"*—woman of shadows. Sometimes in fear. Sometimes in need. Always with caution.

She delivered babies when no doctor would come, nursed dying men through fevers folks said were a punishment from God, and stitched up wounds steadier than most surgeons. She burned sage and sweet grass. Sang under her breath while tying charms from bones and feathers.

Some whispered she was a *voodooienne*, a conjure woman. Others spat the word "witch" and made the sign of the cross when she walked past

But they came to her anyway.

#

People whispered rumors about a pet alligator named Lune, and the chorus of bullfrogs that warned her of intruders. Folks traveled from miles around to knock on her door—not too loud, and never thrice—for healing, for charms, poultices, and tinctures, or to ask questions they were too afraid to voice out loud.

Maman Marie, as some called her, had eyes the color of molasses and a voice like smoked honey. She wore a crown of rosemary and marigold, and her fingers were always stained with herbs. Some said she spoke to ghosts and spirits; others swore she'd once turned a man's heart to stone after he betrayed her.

When babies fell sick and got better overnight, folks claimed that Marie had put "something in the milk." When a man who beat his wife broke out in boils, they whispered that Marie had "looked at him too long." She never defended herself. She let the talk roll off her like river water.

#

Evangeline

One summer evening, when the moon hung low and swollen like a ripe fig, a girl named Evangeline came knocking on the cabin door. Her baby brother had been taken by fever. The town doctor had been perplexed and not been able to help much. Evangeline had pressed through the swamp looking for Maman Marie's unique healing.

The old woman peered into the young girl's eyes, then reached for a bundle of dried rue and a jar filled with fireflies. "You ask for more than healing, chére," she said. "You ask for a door to be opened that God himself may have closed."

"But you talk to the dead," Evangeline pleaded.

Marie sighed and lit a candle made of beeswax and bone. She stirred a pot that hissed and sang in forgotten tongues. That night, under the full moon, she led Evangeline into the swamp with offerings—sugarcane, lilac, and a tear of pure love.

They waited in silence until the wind stopped breathing. Then Evangeline says there came a soft voice—not the baby's, but a woman's, sorrowful and strong: "What was taken cannot always be returned, but love—true love—can ease the ache."

The next morning, the fever broke in Evangeline's brother. He lived. He laughed. And though he never remembered the sickness, he'd often wake crying for a woman he never met.

#

Marie delivered her first baby when she was fourteen—her cousin's, out in a cane shed during a thunderstorm—and never looked back. Over the years, she became Slidell's unofficial healer, midwife, and quiet keeper of old knowledge the church preferred not to acknowledge.

She kept herbs and medicinal odds and ends in the cabin and in a small shack out back: bundles of willow bark, horehound, feverfew, boneset, sassafras, elder, mullein, cat's claw, and roots whose names weren't English or French but old, whispered things from West African or Choctaw mouths. Some she used freely—others only in desperation.

The town didn't talk about Marie's shed. But they came to her door late in the evening or the dark of night, sheepish and whispering:

"My baby's burning up."

"Mama won't stop coughing."

"He can't breathe right come sundown…"

Marie never turned anyone away. She brewed teas, mixed poultices, and burned leaves. She'd mutter words over the fevered, her voice like wind moving through a screen.

But not everyone could risk being seen at her door—not in a place like Slidell, where Sunday gossip could cost a man his job or a woman her reputation.

And that's where Solomon came in.

When families were too ashamed to ask for help, Solomon started leaving bundles of herbs at their doorsteps during the night—just as his mother had taught him. Some knew. Others called it luck. A few thanked God.

But Marie and Solomon knew the truth, and that was enough.

#

Solomon was born twisted and misshapen on a muggy August night. He did not come into the world crying and screaming as other babies do. Instead, Solomon remained silent, like a newborn secret whispered in the wind. His spine was curled like a question mark. His head wasn't shaped like a regular folk. The bones of his skull had grown uneven, bulging at the crown, narrowing near the jaw, as if the Lord had started with a human mold and abandoned it halfway through.

Marie didn't cry. Didn't scream. She held him tenderly to her chest and sang something low and wordless, as if coaxing his soul to stay.

The midwife—young and shaking—asked if she wanted the Last Rites.

Marie simply said: "He's not dying. He's different. That ain't the same thing."

From that night forward, Marie raised Solomon with fierce devotion and the wary vigilance of someone who knew the world would never give her son a fair shake.

15

#

Some said that he came from the swamp itself.

That he was shaped by moss and bark, born under a moon that never rose again, and touched by things that were best left hidden in the darkness of the deep swamp.

#

As he grew older, the deformities became even more noticeable. His brow jutted forward much too far, shadowing eyes that sat too deep and too far apart. They were uneven, with one a bit higher than the other, the lower one having a lid that drooped like it was half-asleep. His nose curved left from birth—never broken, just crooked. His mouth slanted slightly down to the right, even when he tried to smile, which he rarely did.

Hair grew in thick, patchy waves across the back of his head but thinned oddly near the top, leaving a pale spot that glistened with sweat in the sun. His ears, too small for his head, sat too low, giving him a strange, lopsided look—as if someone had stuck them on in the dark.

But it was the shape of the head itself—wide at the crown and narrow at the jaw—that would earn him the cruelest name.

"Onionhead."

#

His mother taught him the names of plants before he could speak full sentences. By five, he could identify dozens of herbs by touch alone. By age ten, he knew how to set bones, steep fever teas, and mix poultices for burns and snakebites.

Most of all, she taught him silence.

16

"The louder you speak, the more they'll twist it. Let the earth speak for you instead."

She heard the unkind things people said about her precious baby boy. "He ain't cursed," she said once, alone in the cabin, speaking only to the wind, as she worked on a curing sachet, placing a newly wrapped bundle of bay leaves and verbena beside her beeswax candle. "He's what's left when mercy and mystery have a child."

#

When Solomon was young, a time when most kids his age were already going to school, he would watch the other children playing in the schoolyard. He would hide near the edge of the woods and watch as they played together, singing children's songs.

He wasn't supposed to be there. He didn't attend the school—no one asked, and his mother didn't offer. But some days, when his chores were done early, he crept through the swamp to the edge of the woods to watch.

He kept low, still, careful not to be noticed. He knew if the teacher saw him—or worse, one of the children—they'd point, maybe shout. Once, they'd thrown a clump of dirt and called him *"bog-born."*

#

Today, he was as quiet as stone.

His eyes followed the turning rope, the cadence, the jumping feet. The song, one of the Willy-the-Wisp rhymes, curled in his ears like smoke. He didn't flinch at the words. He'd heard them before.

... Follow Willy, lose your way,

Mama cries, but you can't stay.

Shows you what you're supposed to be…

He mouthed the lines. His lips didn't make a sound.

In the shadows of the deeper woods behind him, he thought something moved. There was just a flicker—small and blue-white. It hovered, then vanished. No one else seemed to notice. But Solomon did.

He smiled a little, almost shyly, like greeting an old friend.

The game went on. The rope slapped the ground. The chant rose again.

Solomon watched, yearning, not to be the jumper or the singer—but to simply be among them, to belong. He could make toys for them. Little carved rabbits, foxes, snakes, and birds. He left some around town sometimes, on stumps and steps, never asked for thanks. But he always hoped.

The tiny gifts always disappeared.

But nobody ever looked for the giver.

The children kept singing, louder now.

Solomon rose quietly, brushed the leaves from his trousers, and disappeared back into the shadows of the trees.

Behind him, the rope spun, slapping the ground like the steady ticking of a clock.

#

The shallow creek ran off the bayou behind Rosalie Thibodeaux's grand-mère's land. It curled like a crooked arm, half-hidden under scrub oak and water hemlock. Dragonflies flitted like sparks. It was a quiet place, and that was why she came.

She knelt at the bank, collecting acorn caps. She was trying to make whistles out of them—her Pawpaw had taught her how, back when he still remembered names. But her acorn whistles often wheezed more like old lungs.

Across the water, something moved. A rustle. A boy—not much older than her—stooped beneath a tupelo tree, gathering leaves with the slow, sure hands of someone who knew what each one did. His head was large and bulbous at the top, narrow at the jaw. His ears sat too far back. But it wasn't just that. It was the way he moved, like he was listening to things most folks didn't.

"You makin' tea?" she called.

He froze, one hand still outstretched. Eyes wide. Then he lowered the leaf and stared at her like she was a ghost.

"My mama says your mama knows the swamp," Rosalie said. "That you leave bundles for sick folks. You helped my baby brother when he got a bad fever."

No answer.

She lifted one of her acorn caps. "You want one?"

He stepped forward slowly, like he wasn't sure she was real.

"You blow into it gentle, like this." She demonstrated. It made a soft squeal.

He took the cap, turned it in his fingers. His lips parted.

"You talk funny," he said.

19

"You look funny," she replied, smiling. "But I guess that means we match."

And something like the ghost of a grin crossed his face.

They sat near the water for a long time. He didn't speak again, but he carved something into a stick with a knife he pulled from a cord around his neck. She practiced her whistles. The silence between them was warm, not awkward.

When she left, he didn't say goodbye, but he watched her walk all the way back to the path.

#

Solomon held the tin pail with both hands. It was too heavy for his arms, but he wouldn't let his mother carry it today. She had enough to do, and the river roots had been bad on her joints.

The cobbler's porch sat crooked on sun-bleached planks, its shadow stretching across the dirt. He stepped up carefully, careful not to slosh the water inside.

"Boy, what you doin' with that head out in public?" A voice came behind him.

Laughter followed. Several boys, maybe a few years older. The kind that walked in clusters and never alone. One kicked a rock toward Solomon's boots.

"He's gonna drown in that pail if he looks over it," another jeered. "You carryin' water or lookin' for your reflection?"

Solomon flinched but didn't turn. He stepped toward the cobbler's window.

Then—*clang*—the back of his pail was kicked.

The water sloshed out in a rush across the porch boards, splashing his trousers and soaking his shoes.

The boys howled.

"You did that on purpose!" came a bark from inside—Mr. Weller, the cobbler.

Solomon froze.

"You're not to make messes out here. Go on. Out with you."

He opened his mouth to speak, but no words came. His face burned—not with anger, but shame. The kind that sinks into your ribs and stays there.

He picked up the pail, now empty, and stepped down without a word. The boys didn't follow. They didn't need to. They simply ran off—laughing and poking at each other.

By the time Solomon reached the tree line, his cheeks were moist with sweat, yet not a tear had fallen—because Solomon had long since learned how not to cry.

#

As a young boy, Solomon sometimes went to the store for his mother. She let him go because the store was not far from the cabin trail. Today, he carried a few pennies for lye soap. While waiting at the counter, he stared longingly at a jar of taffy—thick, wax-wrapped pieces that glimmered in the light like little miracles.

Mrs. Beulah, the storekeeper's wife, saw him staring.

She was a wide woman with hands like dough and a face folded into a thousand soft wrinkles. Most folks didn't think much of her—too nosy and too loud—but she had a way of seeing things others didn't.

21

When Solomon handed her his pennies, eyes still fixed on the candy jar, she slid the bar of soap across—and added one pale piece of taffy.

"Looks like this one fell in with the groceries," she said with a wink.

Solomon looked up, startled. "I didn't—"

"I know," she said. "Don't you worry. It's between me and the jar."

He took it with both hands, nodding hard, eyes too full for a thank you.

She didn't tell anyone. She never mentioned it again.

But every time he came to the store after that, there was a piece of taffy by the register, just sitting there—like it had gotten lost and was waiting for someone crooked to come set it straight.

#

The grass was wet this cool Fall morning. Solomon's shoes squelched as he walked along the tracks. Sometimes the rocks were uneven and slipped as he walked.

Up ahead, three boys waited—Gervais Boudreaux, a year older and twice as mean—stood by the tracks, arms folded. Beside him were two others: Jules Rousseau and Lionel Cormier. Lionel didn't look up right away.

Solomon slowed, his back already aching from the walk. He knew that look in Jules' eyes—sharp and full of performance.

"Where you goin', twistback?" Gervais called, grinning.

Solomon didn't answer.

Gervais stepped in front of him. "You gotta pay toll if you wanna pass."

Lionel looked down at his feet, mumbling something too soft and gentle to be understood.

Solomon tried to go around, but Gervais sidestepped to block him. Jules picked up a pinecone and lobbed it underhand— it bounced off Solomon's hip. Gervais laughed.

"Careful, Jules, you'll bend him even more than God already did."

The boys laughed. Lionel shifted his feet, softly kicking a small rock near his foot.

Solomon said nothing. Just lowered his eyes and stepped into the weeds. It was muddy here, and the mud sucked at his boots.

"Hey," Gervais called after him. "Say hi to the devil when you see him crawlin' through them trees tonight."

The mud was halfway up Solomon's calves by the time he crawled out of the weeds. His hands trembled, but he didn't cry. Not in front of them.

He walked another half mile in silence, staring at his shadow, not looking back.

#

As time passed, Solomon continued to visit the school. He still wasn't allowed inside. Mrs. Bergeron, the schoolteacher, told him that he was a distraction. He sat beneath the cypress tree at the edge of the schoolyard, legs folded beneath him, drops of sweat on top of his head. His small knife moved like it had memory—thin shavings of pine falling about his boot like curled

23

petals. The wood was soft and yellow, easy to shape. His fingers knew where the rabbit's ears would be before the blade touched them.

This was how he stayed quiet. How he stayed safe.

By carving.

By *making*.

He didn't go near the children. Not because his momma warned him—though she had, in her own way- but because he knew better. They didn't speak to him unless the teacher was watching. They didn't kick him or spit like the other older boys had once done, not anymore. But they didn't ask him to play either. They looked through him, past him, like he was something the eyes didn't quite want to focus on.

But they took the little wooden toys.

He placed the finished rabbit on a flat rock by the playground. The week before it had been a crow. Before that, a coiled snake with tiny eyes, smooth and polished. He never said which child it was for. He just left them where they could be found.

And they always were.

He once saw Annie May Foudre, the baker's daughter, pick one up—a cat with a bent tail. She didn't smile, but she didn't throw it down either. She wiped off some dust on its back and slipped it into her apron.

It was enough.

#

The Tincture Jar

The first time Rosalie set foot into the Moreau cabin, she was clutching a jar of sugar and a letter from her mother that said simply:

Please, if you have something for the cough. — L.T.

Rosalie had expected a hag. She'd heard whispers at school—some children said Marie Moreau could turn people into frogs, or that she fed Solomon swamp water instead of milk when he was a baby. But Rosalie's mother spoke of Marie with a complicated reverence: the kind reserved for people the town needed but didn't trust.

Inside the cabin, the air was heavy and alive. Herbs hung from the rafters like chandeliers of moss and color. Glass jars lined the walls, full of roots and powders, with tiny scrawled labels:

Woundwort. Rue. Castor.

The names looked like spells.

Marie stood by the hearth, not tall but solid. Her hair was wrapped in a faded scarf, and her skirt brushed the floor like a broom.

"You brought payment?" she asked, glancing at the jar of sugar.

Rosalie nodded. "And a note."

Marie opened the letter with hands that looked more like tree bark than flesh. After reading it, she folded it once and slipped it into her pocket.

"She's smart to send you," Marie said. "Folk are less likely to spit at a child."

Rosalie didn't know how to answer that.

Marie turned to the shelf and began mixing from jars, moving with the easy grace of someone who'd done it thousands of times. She said nothing for a long while, then handed Rosalie a small corked bottle. The liquid inside was the color of tobacco and smelled like cinnamon and rain.

"Three drops in tea. Once in the morning, once at night. No more."

Rosalie took it carefully. "What's in it?"

Marie raised an eyebrow. "Why you want to know?"

"I like the way your jars look," Rosalie said. "They remind me of old stories."

Marie smiled at that—not wide, but real.

"Want to see a tincture steep?"

Rosalie nodded so fast she nearly dropped the bottle.

Marie poured hot water over bark and leaves in a small glass. The scent rose like something waking up.

"This here's red clover," Marie said. "Pulls the heaviness out of your chest. This—" she tapped another jar "—mullein. Grows in dry places. Good for lungs. I dry the leaves, but the root's useful too. You know how to tell mullein from dock?"

Rosalie shook her head, eyes wide.

Marie crouched beside her, pointed to the leaf shape. "Dock's bitter in the back of your throat. Mullein's soft like lamb's ears. You remember that, you'll remember the difference."

Rosalie said nothing, but the words carved themselves into her mind.

When she finally stepped back outside, the air felt colder than before. Marie stood in the doorway behind her and said:

"You come back, you bring your own jar."

#

Sometimes Solomon carved in the quiet hours before dawn, when the frogs still called and Marie softly hummed her not-English songs over boiling leaves. She said the gift came from her mother's side— "fingers that know how to pull shape from silence." But Solomon didn't care where it came from. Only that when he carved, he disappeared. His crooked left arm didn't ache. The sideways looks faded. The world quieted.

One of the few times he ever spoke to anyone from town, it was early, and he was sitting along the train tracks, just outside the bushes and trees. A little boy named Jacob Vann came wandering along tracks, checking the plants and bushes, probably searching for lizards or bugs—like a lot of other kids did. As young Jacob came closer, watching from the other side of the tracks, he saw Solomon shaping a bird's wing.

"Why you make 'em?" Jacob asked, squinting to see better, and coming closer.

Solomon looked up, startled. No one had asked before.

He opened his mouth. Paused.

"Because hands remember," he finally said, though he wasn't sure the boy would understand.

Jacob just shrugged. "That one's pretty."

Solomon nodded and held it out.

The boy hesitated—but took it and ran off without a thank you.

The next day, that bird sat tucked in Jacob's shirt pocket. Solomon saw it when the boy reached up to scratch his neck.

He didn't say anything.

He never did.

###

4. THE NAME THEY GAVE HIM

Days later, the school let out early, and he lingered outside the schoolyard. He was sitting behind an old live oak with its gnarled roots and cicada-thick bark. He had found some sassafras nearby and was tying a small satchel of sassafras bark closed when he heard them—three boys, still dawdling, just out of sight on the other side of the oak.

"Why he always crouched like that?"

"Looks like a frog waitin' to boil."

"Nah, look at that head—swear to God, looks like an *onion*!"

Laughter burst through the air like a firecracker, sharp and thoughtless.

"Onionhead! That's what he is. Onionhead Moreau!"

More laughter. One boy, Gervais, stepped around the tree and saw Solomon sitting there, still and blinking.

"Hey, Onionhead," he said, grinning wide. "Ain'tcha got any spell to fix that squash you call a skull?"

The others followed, throwing small pebbles and pinecones—not hard, not to hurt, just to sting. Just to humiliate.

Solomon didn't speak. He couldn't. His throat had gone tight, like it was cinched with a thread.

He didn't cry either. He just stood slowly, taller than the boys expected, his misshapen head catching the last slant of sun like a cracked porcelain bowl.

He looked at them—just looked—and something in his eye, ancient and unblinking, made them stop laughing.

Then he turned and walked into the woods.

The nickname would follow him from that day on, sticking like burrs in dry cotton. He decided not to say a word about this to his mother, although it was on his mind the whole walk home.

When he got home, he placed the sassafras bark gently on the windowsill, next to the candle she kept lit when he stayed out past supper. She saw it when she came in from tending to a neighbor's sick baby.

She never asked why he was quiet that night.

But she did sit beside him on the porch in silence, and when the wind picked up through the trees, she laid her hand on his shoulder—not to comfort, not to fix, not to witness.

And that meant more than any spell.

#

"Onionhead."

It started with the schoolboys. By the time he was eleven, even grown men said it with a kind of rough humor, nudging each other with grins and smirks. Some used it openly, like it was his Christian name.

"Watch out, Onionhead's out by the mill."

"Don't let Onionhead look at the baby."

"He's got bad blood in that bulb-shaped skull of his. Born touched."

He never responded to it. He never looked up when they said it. He just walked—limping slightly from one hip, the result of a malformed pelvis—and kept his eyes on the ground. But he heard it. He always heard it.

Children were warned to stay away from him and never go to the moss-veiled cabin in the woods. Some people crossed the road when they saw him coming. Others threw stones.

Despite everything, Solomon never struck back. He never raised his voice, never cursed them. He tended the plants in his mother's garden, collected more from nature, and laid out herbs for the sick like quiet prayers wrapped in twine.

He couldn't change the shape of his skull. Couldn't smooth the thick joints of his hands or reshape the slope of his shoulders. But he could choose silence over bitterness.

And he did.

Every single day.

#

It was Sunday morning, hot even in the shade, and Solomon—age twelve, now—stood outside St. Jude's Church in town with a paper fan in his hand, waiting.

The other children had already gone inside. The pews were full of pressed linen and tight collars. The smell of soap and sweat hung in the air. Hymns drifted out the windows like smoke.

Solomon stood by the side door. He didn't go by the main entrance anymore. Not since the time Mrs. Allemond grabbed her daughter's arm and said, "We don't need bad omens sitting beside us."

So, he sat at the side door, staring at the painted white steps, chipped and dirt-streaked.

He wanted to hear the singing up close. Wanted to feel the wood of the pew under his palms. He wanted to be inside, like everyone else. He wanted to bow his head like the others.

31

But when he'd asked his momma if he could sit in the front row once, she'd smiled sad and said, "Maybe best you just listen from outside, sugar."

So, he did.

He sat on the side stoop, the wood warm beneath him, and let the music wash over his shoulders like river water. It made his back ache less. Made the days feel shorter.

Sometimes he hummed along.

When church let out, he stood and waited for everyone to leave before heading home, dust clinging to his bare arms, heart full and sore at the same time.

#

The school bell had long since rung to go home, but a cluster of children still lingered near the old magnolia tree behind the clapboard building. The girls played jacks in the dirt, skirts tucked around their knees. The boys circled each other with pockets full of marbles and mischief.

A few of them had started a game—one that didn't have rules, exactly, just a chant and some pointing at each other.

"Walk like Onionhead!"

"Talk like Onionhead!"

Laughter erupted as a boy named Eli LeClerc hunched his shoulders and dragged one leg behind him, lips parted in a crooked grin, eyes wide in an exaggerated stare. The others howled with glee, stomping their feet and hooting.

One girl, Josie Lang, clutched a wooden doll to her chest and whispered, "Mama says he's got swamp blood. Mama says his bones didn't grow right 'cause he wasn't meant to be born."

32

Another child chimed in, "My brother said his mama talks to snakes and calls the wind."

They all turned toward the woods beyond the fence line, where trees pressed close together like they were hiding secrets. For a moment, no one spoke.

Then someone said, "Bet he sleeps in a coffin," and the laughter started again, nervous this time, like they all felt something cold crawl up their backs but didn't dare admit it.

#

The sky was thick with mosquitoes and moonlight when Marie came back from delivering a fever tonic to the Blanchet twins. Sol sat at the kitchen table, sorting dried mullein and yarrow into jars, his fingers slow and careful.

She noticed the silence first. No hum under his breath. No soft sniffing of the herbs like he usually did. Just the sound of clinking, and lids being tightened too hard.

She didn't ask right away.

Instead, she poured them both some chicory coffee—his half milk—and handed him a sugar biscuit left from market day.

They ate in silence until she said, without looking up:

"What they call you, bébé?"

Sol didn't answer.

She didn't press. Just waited, sipping slowly.

After a long while, he took a deep breath and whispered:

"Onionhead."

Marie blinked once. Then again. Her mouth stayed in a tight line. She reached across the table and cupped his chin, tilting his face gently toward the oil lamp.

"You listen to me, Solomon Moreau. There ain't a damn thing wrong with how God shaped you. Your head is full of knowing, full of watchin', full of things this world too small to understand. They call you 'Onionhead' like it's a curse. But onions, they grow underground, where folks don't notice. They take root. And when you cut 'em—they make people cry."

She paused.

"That means you carry power, *mon petit*. More than they got."

Sol blinked fast, throat tight.

Marie kissed the top of his head—the high part, the part that always caught stares—and whispered something in old French, too soft to catch.

He never forgot that night.

#

The Girl Who Saw Him

One afternoon, under a mostly blue sky with white cottony clouds drifting slowly on their way to somewhere else, Solomon sat by the cypress near the schoolyard, carving a small wooden bird with a pointed beak, a wren. A girl named Mira watched him sitting there working. She'd seen some of the other animals he'd carved. She slowly walked up, like a kitten, unsure of what it was seeing, unsure whether to be strong or scared.

"Did you carve all those little things?" she asked.

Solomon nodded but did not speak.

"They're beautiful," she said, and meant it.

Every day, Solomon came to sit under the cypress, and Mira returned. She sat and talked. Well, Mira talked. Solomon sat carving, occasionally nodding or making a little grunt at something she said. She never mentioned his face or how he looked.

One afternoon, Mira sat talking in her typical one-sided way. Some of the children watched, as they had for days. One boy whispered—loud enough to be heard by the cypress—something cruel. The other children laughed. Some pointed. Mira stood and said, loud enough for all to hear: "*He carves better animals than you'll ever be.*"

The laughter stopped.

And though not everyone changed, Solomon walked a bit straighter from that day on—not because his spine had healed, but because someone had seen the beauty behind his crooked smile.

\#

The bell above the door jingled as Mabel Fontenot stepped into the general store, wiping sweat from her brow with a lace handkerchief. Inside, the air was still thick and close, despite the cross-breeze. Three women stood near the flour sacks, fanning themselves and swapping stories that had long since stretched the truth into something more satisfying.

"You know she only comes to town when the moon's wrong," said Irene Toussaint, voice low but sharp.

"Her and that boy," added another, "never say a word unless you ask 'em twice. And even then, he just stares at you like he can see under your skin."

35

Mabel leaned in. "My cousin swears she saw Marie Moreau burying something in the hollow stump behind the chapel. Said it was wrapped in cloth, smelled like vinegar and rot."

Irene clucked her tongue. "That boy's not right. I don't care what anyone says. He's got something crawling in him. Gave my youngest one of those little wooden things—whittled like a rabbit, only the eyes were too big. I threw it in the stove. Didn't even burn proper."

A silence fell over them. Only the squeak of the ceiling fan filled the space for a moment.

Then, as if summoned by the dark mood, the bell above the door jingled again.

But it was just Marshal Kincaid, wiping his forehead, looking for coffee.

Still, none of the women resumed their gossip—not until he passed.

And not one of them would say it aloud, but the unspoken truth between them pulsed like a second heartbeat: *Something was wrong with that boy.*

#

The loft above his mother's herb shed was a refuge of sorts. The smells of fresh and dry herbs, some sweet, some pungent, filled the shed. It was like an overload of nature rushing into his senses. Solomon would climb up and lie on the boards between the rafters. Shirt off, one arm under his head, staring at the cracked roof beams like they might give him answers.

He wasn't strong, but he worked like he was—doing odd jobs when he could find them. It made his back scream, made his hip ache. But he never let anyone see.

This afternoon, he overheard two boys in town—the Duval twins—laughing near the blacksmith's shop about "that crooked boy out in the Moreau woods," saying how he'd probably die with his head twisted backward like in a possum trap.

Solomon didn't respond. He just walked past them like the wind through dry grass. But his ears burned.

He climbed the ladder to the loft that night and didn't come down till morning.

Lying there in the dark, he clenched his jaw and whispered to the beams above him.

"One day I'll be gone, and y'all can talk to the trees. See if they answer back."

He meant it, too.

Not out of hate.

Just a deep, aching certainty that no one in town would ever truly want him to stay.

#

Even at sixteen, Solomon only came to town when he needed to, face turned downward, body hunched from more than just his crooked spine. The tinsmith, Mr. Felix Rudd, was old and mostly deaf, but sharp-eyed and clever with his hands.

Solomon brought him a kettle lid to fix. He waited, silent.

Rudd looked up, squinting.

"You, Marie's boy?"

Solomon nodded.

Rudd looked him over—long head, heavy brow, deep-set eyes—and then grinned.

37

"Got a head like an old-time melon. Don'tcha? All the best folks do."

Solomon flinched slightly.

"Means you hold more thinkin' than the rest of us. Good. World needs someone to do the hard rememberin'."

Solomon stared, stunned.

Rudd didn't joke. Didn't sneer.

He just fixed the lid and handed it back, tapping Solomon's wrist gently.

"You come back anytime. My shop's got no use for cowards."

Solomon left without saying a word, but he held that kettle lid like it was a silver medal.

###

5. DARKENING SKIES

Her name was Mary-Ellen Ledoux, just five years old, with hair the color of ripening strawberries and a laugh like dandelion fluff. She was the youngest of three, the only girl, and her father—Joseph Ledoux, who worked at the Slidell train depot—always said she was the only thing that could quiet a room without saying a word.

Mary-Ellen was the kind of child who liked small things—pebbles, marbles, bottle caps. She kept them in a rusted Altoids tin tucked in her dress pocket, collecting the world one tiny trinket at a time. She had a habit of singing to herself, half-formed songs with no rhyme or reason. The other children didn't play with her as much, not because she was odd, but because she seemed to be content alone, dancing under the magnolia trees like she belonged more to the wind than to the earth.

#

The town of Slidell woke on a Sunday morning to heat that clung like wet wool and the slow, steady hum of cicadas vibrating against the windows of St. Jude's Church. Reverend Landry's voice drifted over the congregation, but folks were distracted. The Ledoux pew was half-empty. Folks fanned themselves with songbooks, children in suspenders and hand-sewn dresses squirmed in the pews. Mothers nodded toward them with tight smiles and tired eyes.

Mrs. Ledoux sat pale on the far-right bench, her hands twisting the hem of her skirt. Little Mary-Ellen wasn't there in her sky-blue dress and Sunday boots. Her mother, Adéle, sat rigid beside an empty space, her eyes glassy and distant. Someone whispered the child hadn't come home the night before.

That she'd gone to pick wildflowers and never returned. It wasn't the first time she had gone missing.

At first, it was nothing. Mary-Ellen was prone to wandering, maybe out to the train platform to see some stray kittens in a box behind the general store or off exploring for the tiny bits that she always collected.

By suppertime, there was no sign of her. Her father called for her up and down the street, hands cupped to his mouth. Her mother searched the back lot behind their house, looked in ditches, and shouted her name until her voice cracked. Some of the neighbors joined in, and they searched late into the night.

The next morning was Sunday. Her mother had stayed sitting on the front steps of their house all night long, her father in a chair just inside the door. The decision was made to go to church, in the hope that Mary-Ellen would be there. Reverand Landry paused halfway through the second verse of *Nearer, My God, to Thee.* Services ended early, and search parties formed.

By the time the Sun was beginning to settle in for the night, search parties had grown to half the town. A creeping dread had settled over the town like smoke. In the dying light, lanterns were lit. People searched along fence lines and into the pinewoods. Voices echoed through town, *"Mary-Ellen!"* like the name itself might guide her home.

#

A group of volunteers had been walking the tracks, fanning out in pairs—some with dogs, others with sticks to push back brush. Marshal Kincaid was among them, grey-faced and hollow-eyed, having helped search the night before. They hadn't found a damn thing in town. Not a footprint. Not a ribbon. Not a trail.

It was old Sam Tolbert who saw her first—old man Sam, who pushed a cart full of scrap and bottles up and down the tracks every morning. Folks said he talked to himself, but in the fading light, he said nothing at all. Just stood there, frozen, staring down the tracks like he'd seen the Devil himself.

#

The Body

They found her along the tracks, half hidden where the gravel turned to grass. Nearby was the place where hobos sometimes camped. A place where children were not supposed to play. She lay curled on her side in the gravel, as if she'd lain down to sleep, but her dress—white with pink and red flowers—was ripped and torn apart, only in pieces streaked and stained with dirt and blood. Her legs were bare. Her shoes were missing. Her hair, once braided and tied with bright red ribbons—now pulled loose from the braids—matted and streaked with mud.

One hair ribbon was caught in some nearby brambles. There was no sign of the other.

Her eyes were open.

She was not sleeping.

By the time Marshal Kincaid got there, a small crowd was already gathering. He said nothing when he saw her. He tipped his hat back and knelt beside her, his shadow stretching long over the stones in the dying light. She'd been brutalized—her body left like something discarded.

The marshal reached down and brushed a bit of dirt from her cheek. Her eyes stared past him toward the evening sky. He gently closed them with trembling fingers.

Two other men approached, then stopped short, stepping back like they'd touched a hot stove. One crossed himself. The other looked away, swallowing hard.

"Who'd do this to a baby girl?" one of the men whispered.

No one answered.

The marshal didn't have the words. He took off his hat and looked up at the sky. He'd seen men shot. Drowned. Hanged. But this was different. This was...*wrong*.

"What in God's name . . ." someone whispered.

"Oh, Jesus." Said another.

She'd been there since yesterday. There was a large open wound along the hairline above her left temple. Blood had turned her normally strawberry hair into a deep rusty red. The girl's neck had been slashed deep. Too deep. A bloody handprint could be seen where her neck joined her body, like a scarlet misshapen necklace. Her hands were bruised; she had fought. Her fingers, tiny and dirt-caked, were curled in a death grip around a broken piece of porcelain from the head of a doll—Miss Penelope. Everyone knew Mary-Ellen never went anywhere without her. Only a broken half-face of the doll was left.

#

In the brambles under the ribbon, almost hidden in the grass, weeds, and briars—half-sunken in mud—someone noticed a small wooden figure.

One of Solomon's carved animals.

A small wooden dog. The kind he whittled and gave to children around town. Each one is different. This one lacked his usual craftsmanship. It had a chipped ear, and there were tiny initials carved into the base: **S.M.**

"That's his," someone whispered.

The marshal squatted by the thicket, picked up the wooden figure. Turned it over in his hand.

He was sure Solomon had made it.

Kincaid rose, his jaw tight. "Send someone back to town. Get her mother. Don't say too much—just enough to get her to come quiet. And somebody tell that mob to get their asses out of the swamp!"

#

People grieved together, holding each other because it was all they could do. Mothers held their children close. Shopkeepers locked their doors. People walked slowly down the center of the street, silent and dazed. No one shouted. No one cried out loud.

The silence was worse.

Food was brought to the Ledoux house. Candles lit. Prayers said.

But soon—all too soon—the sorrow would turn to something else.

The railroad had once made this town. Now it felt like it cursed it.

#

The news rolled through Slidell before dawn the next day— quiet at first, then louder. The marshal was on the tracks, scrawling notes. Preacher Landry rang the church bell at sunup,

43

not for worship, but to let the people know that God is present and watching over them.

Children were kept indoors. Mothers held them too tightly. The grocer refused to open. Everyone had a theory. Everyone had a suspect.

Some said it was a rail-rider who had jumped a train. Others claimed it was a big swamp cat that had wandered close to town and become too bold. One boy claimed that he had seen her walking near the Moreau woods, talking to the air.

Rumors, superstition, and fear grew teeth.

By mid-afternoon, no one was working, no children were playing, and the well in front of the town hall stood deserted. Grief rolled through Slidell, not like thunder, but like a slow, rising flood. The kind of sorrow that seeps into walls, into stitching, into the marrow of bones.

###

6. IT BEGINS TO RAIN

Dark clouds moved overhead in a slow dance of building fury. It was long after sun-up the next day, but the gloom from the clouds kept the sunlight at bay, throwing everything into the ever-present shadow. People gathered around the town hall, which also housed the marshal's office and jails in a separate section.

Word had gotten around that Onionhead had been seen near Widow Carrow's livestock pen the night her prize goat had vanished.

She was ranting now, loud and shaking.

"He walks crooked and talks to plants! I saw him with them charms and bones! Y'all know he ain't right."

#

Marie was there, in town, delivering an herb packet for a sickly child. She stepped out from the back of the crowd, slow and straight-backed in her indigo skirt and wide-brim hat.

"You gonna blame my son for every shadow you can't explain?"

A peal of thunder rumbled through, growing in the distance and rolling over the crowd like a shudder from the sky.

The crowd stilled.

"Your goats got taken by coyotes, not curses. And if Solomon had intended to do you harm, you wouldn't have any goats left at all."

Gasps.

She stepped closer, right up to Widow Carrow.

"You lookin' for someone to burn. But you'd best make sure they carry fire, not healing."

There was a sudden burst of lightning that illuminated the crowd like the flash of a camera, saving the image for posterity. Thunder roared like an angry beast—seeming to last forever.

Nobody said another word.

The sky opened, dropping a deluge of water onto the crowd and the town. People ran for cover. Everyone except Marie. She stood stone still for a while, only turning her head slightly to watch folks run from nature. After everyone had cleared the street, some watching from inside nearby buildings, she straightened her wide-brimmed hat and slowly walked away.

There was still a sick child in need of her help.

\#

At the cabin, the sky broke open with no warning. No slow build. No whisper of wind.

Just a great shudder of lightning, like God cracked his knuckles over the swamp.

Solomon had felt it coming. Not through thunder or clouds, but through the sudden stillness of the trees, the way the herons had flown inland in tight, low arcs, wings like knives against the sky.

He had just finished binding a fever root bundle for old Miss Dupré's rheumatism when the first crack hit—loud enough to make the jars rattle on the shelves, and one fell with a crash.

Rain came sideways, hard and thick as muscadine vines. It slapped the roof in sheets, found its way through the warped boards in cold streams that trickled down the walls. The swamp outside groaned, alive and restless, the bayou water swelling against its edges.

Solomon moved like a man in ritual. Calm. Steady. He stuffed rags into the windowsills, lit two more oil lamps, and poured salt across the doorway. Then he unwrapped the black cloth from the old mirror.

He never did that.

But tonight, the storm felt different.

Marie always said some tempests weren't just weather, but visitations. That certain storms came to wash the rot from the soul. Or to demand something long overdue.

He stood in front of the mirror and looked.

It hit him like a body blow—the reflection. That long, heavy brow, the too-wide mouth, the skull misshapen and lopsided. The name whispered back to him like an echo:

Onionhead.

But Marie's voice rose louder.

"You're marked, yes—but not by the devil—by me. By the women who came before me. You carry a shape this world doesn't know how to love—but it's not meant for them. It's meant for the earth."

He sank to the floor.

All around him, the storm roared—an orchestra of wrath. Water tore through the roof in a dozen places now, soaking herbs and floorboards, knocking over candles. The wind screamed through the eaves, and something outside—maybe a tree, maybe worse—snapped with a great, splintering groan.

Solomon didn't run. He didn't flinch.

Instead, he sang.

A low, old tune in broken Creole, taught to him by Marie in the cradle. A storm song. A lullaby for spirits and children.

He sang until the wind answered him.

He sang until the rain eased its fists.

He sang until he believed his own voice.

By morning, half the roof was gone.

But the mirror still stood.

And Solomon Moreau—*Onionhead*—was still breathing.

#

What the Water Brought

Outside the cabin, the world smelled of rain and decay.

The storm had passed like a fever, leaving behind a hush that felt reverent, like the pause after a prayer. Solomon stepped barefoot onto the porch of his battered cabin, its planks soft and spongy with water, roof half-caved above his sleeping corner.

Birdsong had not yet returned.

Even the frogs were quiet.

He made his way slowly down the sodden steps, hand trailing along the railing where his mother dried bundles of lemon balm and rue. The path to the waterline had vanished, swallowed by the rising bayou, now a wide mirror of still, brown water.

And at the edge—where root met flood—something moved.

At first, Solomon thought it was driftwood. A long, pale tangle caught on the roots of a toppled cypress.

But as he neared, he saw it wasn't wood at all.

It was a child's doll.

Porcelain face, half-smashed. One eye missing. Hair of dark yarn was soaked and clinging to its scalp like seaweed. Its cotton dress—white once, now gray—was caught on a branch, fluttering like a little drowned ghost.

Solomon froze.

He knew that doll.

It had belonged to Mary-Ellen Ledoux, the little girl they'd found by the tracks. He remembered the tiny lace hem from the day her mother carried her into town last spring, clinging to that doll like a lifeline. It had been all the talk when she went missing. People called it *"a beloved toy, likely taken by the killer."*

But this was miles from the tracks. Miles from the search parties.

Miles from any path someone might've taken by accident.

Solomon knelt beside it, mud soaking into his pants. He touched the doll with trembling fingers.

Not an accident.

Not nature.

He looked up. The trees were silent. But he could feel eyes—many, unseen—watching from the greenery beyond. The swamp had *delivered something*, just as it had always done for his mother. But this time, it wasn't healing.

It was a warning.

Or a clue.

The wind stirred the moss above him. Somewhere, far off, a hawk screamed.

Solomon stood and gently wrapped the doll in a square of cloth. He didn't know what he was meant to do with it yet. Someone had been near his home. Someone who wanted him to know. Know what?

And now the storm wasn't over.

Not truly.

It had only just begun.

#

Dr. Bergeron sat in silence, elbows on his knees, staring at the little girl's ruined body on the table. A thin cotton sheet covered her midsection and legs, but the bruises, the swelling along her throat, the fractured skull, and the broken collarbone told the story clearly enough.

He adjusted his spectacles. Took a long breath.

The room smelled of camphor, sweat, and blood that had already turned to rust.

He had seen death. Had seen pneumonia twist the lungs, seen tetanus lock a body like iron. But this…

This was *deliberate*.

Not an accident. Not a fall.

The fracture on her temple had the clean edge of a blunt strike—low and fast. Not the strength of a boy. Not even a panicked child. No. It came from above, angled downward. Someone taller. Someone who *knew how hard to hit to kill*.

Then there were the marks on her neck, other than the deep cut—a cut that reached down to her windpipe. There were pressure points—bruising—under the jaw. A handprint. Broad.

He stood, circled the table again.

And then—at her side—he spotted it. A small splinter of cedar. Nearly missed it in the gauze folds. He plucked it gently with tweezers and turned it over in the lamplight.

It smelled faintly of smoke.

He turned the splinter in his palm and thought of the tiny carved animals he'd seen before. He remembered a fox on a windowsill in the Weller house. A bird with wings outstretched at the church. Always elegant. Always peaceful.

Dr. Bergeron frowned. Something didn't sit right.

They had found a small wooden dog nearby.

If Solomon had left it, why leave such an odd piece?

And more than that—Solomon's hands were skilled, but not strong. Could he even swing a blow like the one Mary-Ellen had taken?

He sighed. Locked it all away in a drawer. He wasn't the marshal. Wasn't a judge or jury. And if he spoke now—if he said the town might be wrong—he'd be lucky to keep his license, let alone his life.

Still…
He felt the truth hanging in the air like storm humidity.

"It's not him," he whispered.

"But they'll kill him anyway."

#

Solomon held the doll in both hands, as if it might wake if jostled too roughly.

It was small—no bigger than a baby possum—its limbs limp and wet, but not soaking wet. The porcelain face was cracked like an old teacup, one painted blue eye staring glassily at the sky, the other lost to time. Its mouth was a faint red curve, chipped at the corner as if it had once been trying to speak and failed.

The dress had been fine once—white muslin with pale blue ribbon and tiny lace trim—but now it was discolored by dirty water and ash-colored with swamp rot. A line of neat stitching, hand-sewn, ran across the shoulder. Someone, likely the girl's mother, had mended it with loving care. But now the threads were coming loose, waving like little white tendrils in the breeze.

There were no footprints near the waterline.

No scuff of a boot or broken branch.

No sign of anyone passing by.

Just the doll—as if the flood had delivered it straight from death's hands.

Solomon stared at the thing for a long while. He remembered hearing how people had searched for it even after the body was found. Mary-Ellen's mother had walked along the tracks weeping, calling the doll's name as if it might come running home.

But that was days ago. The tracks were miles away. And the doll was dry beneath the outer layer of muck. Not fresh, not recently dropped. It hadn't floated in that night from town.

It had come from somewhere deeper.

Somewhere darker.

And maybe not alone.

Solomon felt the hair rise on his arms.

He looked up. The cypress trees were still; there was no wind. Spanish moss dangled low like the fingers of drowned spirits. Insects should have been singing, frogs should have been calling—but there was only the distant groan of the shifting swamp, like something old turning over in its sleep.

He smelled something then—not rot, not swamp gas, but roses. Faint and fleeting, like a memory caught in a draft.

His mother used to say the dead left signs when they weren't finished speaking.

"Sometimes they send back what they touched last. A shawl. A shoe. A name carved where no hand's been."

Solomon didn't know what the doll meant yet. But he knew this: it hadn't arrived by accident. Nor by human hands.

And when he held it to his chest, he swore it gave off a faint warmth—just for a moment, like a child pressing its face into his shirt.

#

The doctor pronounced it murder, no doubt. No accident. And not a drifter—he said the wounds were deliberate. Familiar. Angry. That meant it was probably someone local. Someone close.

By midday, rumors spread like fire.

Some blamed the traveling men who rode the rails. Others whispered about the butcher's son, who always played rough. Some blamed the Ledoux family themselves—said they were cursed, that Mary-Ellen had been seen talking to shadows near the levee.

But one name came up more than any other.

It was Old Emile who first said his name.

"There's that one in the woods," he muttered. *"The hunchback."*

Everyone knew who he meant.

Solomon Moreau.

"Onionhead!"

Someone said he'd been seen near the tracks the day before. Another swore he'd once chased a cat with a knife. Someone else said he kept *things* in jars.

Truth didn't matter anymore. Not really. The fear had its hooks in.

###

7. FIRE IN THE BLOOD

Mary-Ellen was buried two days later, her tiny coffin barely longer than a sewing bench. They buried her near the center of the graveyard, beneath carved angels and lilies.

The men of the town stood quiet in the back row, hats in hand, eyes hard. Their grief mixed with something darker.

It festered.

By evening, the town square was full.

Lanterns swayed in the night breeze. The church bell rang without a sermon.

#

Tensions Grow

He was a quiet man, strange in his ways but never unkind. Children whispered stories about him—some called him a witchman, others said he talked to owls. But the older folks knew better. He carved walking sticks and tiny toy animals from cypress root, left bundles of herbs on porches when babies were sick. Most folks left him alone.

#

The afternoon after Mary-Ellen was laid to rest, a knot of men stood outside the marshal's office, itching for answers and naming Solomon loud enough to hear through the shutters. No one had seen him the day she had disappeared—but that, to them, was proof enough.

"He's always watching, isn't he?" said Gervais.

"Hiding in them woods," spat Jules.

"Who else could do something like that?"

Marshal Kincaid raised a hand. "There's no evidence," he said. "We don't condemn a man on rumors."

But fear is louder than reason.

Whispers turned to rumors. A drifter had been seen at the rail depot. Someone remembered a stranger asking for water down near Tassin's farm. The marshal rode out and back again, but no one had been arrested. No name written down. Nothing proven.

#

Rosalie

At the cabin, someone knocked.

The knock wasn't on the door.

It was on the *trees*.

A careful, deliberate rap—two times—on the trunk of the cypress just beyond Solomon's clearing. And then again. The way folks used to announce themselves was when they didn't want to step too close.

Solomon was inside, still wrapping the doll in oilcloth, when he heard it. He set it gently on his mother's old chair and stepped out into the hush of the morning.

The visitor waited at the tree line, hat in hand.

Rosalie Thibodeaux.

A young woman, tall and slender with skin the color of pecan wood and eyes like green glass. She was no stranger to the woods—he'd seen her wandering the wild areas most sensible folks avoided, gathering mushrooms or wild garlic, always with a satchel and a quiet kind of purpose. She occasionally came to

Marie to learn about the roots, herbs, and mysteries that nature seldom shared with outsiders.

Most folks in town wouldn't come within shouting distance of the cabin. But Rosalie wasn't most folks. She was one of the few who took the time to talk to Solomon. She was always kind. Kinder than all the rest.

"You an' your mama weather it alright?" she asked, eyes flicking to the broken porch roof, the scattered shingles like dark petals around the cabin.

Solomon nodded once.

Rosalie stepped closer, mud sucking at her boots. Her gaze settled on him, then drifted to the bundled cloth resting on the chair behind him.

"You found something," she said.

It wasn't a question.

Solomon hesitated.

"I was out this morning," she continued. "Checking for downed branches near the stream. And I saw something strange—real strange."

He waited.

"There was a trail," she said. "A thin line of red thread. Hanging from tree to tree, like somebody stitched the air together."

Solomon's jaw tensed.

Rosalie stepped closer now, lowering her voice.

"My gran used to say that meant a spirit was trying to keep its soul from unraveling."

At last, Solomon spoke—his voice rough from disuse.

"You ever hear of a child's doll floatin' uphill?"

Rosalie's brow furrowed.

"I found her this mornin'," Solomon said. "Not near the tracks. Not near town. Just there—on the bank, like she's been waitin'."

Rosalie stepped up onto the porch, slow and reverent, her eyes on the bundle. She didn't reach for it. Didn't ask to touch it.

"You think she sent it?" she asked. "Mary-Ellen?"

Solomon looked past her, into the trees.

"I think somethin' did. Somethin' that still wants speakin'."

The swamp sighed behind them. A bird called once, high and lonely.

Rosalie nodded slowly, crossing herself with one hand and reaching into her satchel with the other. She pulled out a charm—a small bag tied shut with black twine, filled with salt, peppercorns, and dried camphor. She set it on the railing.

"For protection," she said. "You're already half in the veil, Solomon. Just … don't step all the way through without tellin' someone."

She turned and walked back into the trees, boots leaving no mark in the mud. Solomon stood in the doorway long after she was gone, staring down at the doll.

It hadn't moved.

But the cloth around it was damp with something new - rosewater, faint and impossible. A scent not there before.

And in the far trees, a red thread fluttered.

#

The town's grief had curdled into something meaner.

The marshal did what he could—questioned folks, poked around the edges of the woods, but Slidell didn't run on facts. It ran on *feel*. And folks *felt* the killer was still close. Watching. Breathing the same air.

Then a boy named Eddie Bellweather came running into town, out of breath and near crying, shouting that he'd found something behind the schoolhouse—out where the bayou-fed brush grew high, where the kids sometimes dared each other to sneak cigarettes. Not far from an old cypress tree, the one where Onionhead used to sit and carve little animals.

A crowd gathered fast.

It was just past noon, the sun was burning hot, when they saw it.

A piece of Mary-Ellen's dress and a red ribbon—once bright red, now dull and dirty.

Torn.

A ragged piece of torn cloth—white, with pink and red flowers—just like the dress she wore the day she vanished. Caught on the tip of a hawthorn bush.

"How'd that get here?"

"She was found near the tracks."

"And now this?"

And just like that, the quiet unease in town turned sharp.

From porch whispers to shouted certainty.

From suspicion to rage.

#

The sun had just begun to sag behind the cypress trees, casting shadows across the worn dirt road that split Slidell in two. Outside Beulah's General Store, a cluster of townsfolk had gathered, swatting flies and trading words, trying to talk sense into the horror that had taken root since little Mary-Ellen's body was found near the railroad tracks.

The conversation had turned sour.

"He always skulks 'round them woods. Never says a word. Just watchin'," said Marcel Dubois, a mean-spirited man with a jaw like a cracked anvil.

"That boy ain't right," muttered Old Man Tolbert, spitting tobacco near the wheel of his mule cart. "Ain't never been. Walkin' crooked since he come out the womb."

"I seen him starin' at the schoolhouse last week," said Viola Greene, her voice trembling with something half-true and half-fed by fear. "Maybe he was waitin'…"

From the edge of the crowd, a shape stepped forward—a woman in a wide, sun-bleached headwrap and a skirt the color of dried magnolias. Her skin was rich and burnished from years of bayou wind and ash. Her eyes were dark stones, steady and sharp.

Marie Moreau.

And when she spoke, she didn't raise her voice. She didn't have to.

"You will not speak of my son like he's a sickness you can scrub off your doorstep."

The crowd quieted. Even Jules blinked.

"Solomon Moreau has done nothin' but help this town in ways half of you too proud to admit. When your babies were burnin' up and your money was short, who left y'all bundles of herbs? When the Broussard's boy couldn't breathe at night, who laid mullein and marshmallow root on your porch with no name, no price?"

No one answered.

She stepped closer. Her presence, once a whisper, now thick in the air.

"He doesn't speak like you. Don't walk like you. That doesn't make him a monster. That makes him mine. And God doesn't make mistakes with what He gives a mother to carry."

Her voice trembled once—only once—and it wasn't with fear. It was with the terrible strength of someone who had spent too long burying her tenderness under other people's cruelty.

Beulah stood behind the screen door, unmoving, watching. She didn't interrupt.

Marie looked slowly from face to face.

"You want to chase shadows, go look in your own hearts. See what rots there. But if one more person raises a hand to my boy, I swear by every name my grandmother taught me—I'll call on somethin' older than this town, and it will remember how you treated the innocent."

No one met her eyes after that. The crowd began to loosen, drift apart, muttering excuses to themselves as they went.

Only Beulah remained, and when Marie turned to leave, the shopkeeper whispered:

"He's lucky to have you."

Marie didn't smile. She only nodded and walked back into the heat, her head high, her steps slow and sure.

In her wake, the dust didn't settle… it trembled.

#

The townsfolk gathered that evening, not in the church this time, but outside the Ledoux house, candles in hand, some holding back tears, others letting them fall freely. Women brought casseroles and jars of molasses, as if food might patch the hole where Mary-Ellen had been. Men mumbled words like *justice, monster,* and *God help us.*

Mrs. Ledoux didn't speak. She stood on the porch, her face hollow, her husband a ghost beside her. No one knew what to say, but they stood there anyway, because standing together was all they could do.

#

Time stretched on, thick with heat and grief. Slidell was never quite the same. Children were kept close. Strangers were watched from behind lace curtains. And, along the tracks, a small white cross appeared.

The town had gone still. Quiet in the way things get when everyone's thinking the same wicked thought, but no one wants to say it first.

###

8. ASSAULT ON THE CABIN

That same night, four men with shotguns made their way into the woods toward the cabin. The woods held their breath as the men crept up the trail, lanterns bobbing like fireflies behind a funeral procession. No one spoke. The only sounds were the huff of boots over roots and the quiet clink of buckles and cartridge belts. The path to Marie Moreau's cabin wasn't hard to follow; it had been worn down by years of quiet visitors seeking her tonics, teas, and whispered help.

But tonight, no one came for healing.

They came for reckoning.

#

The cabin came into view just as the sky bruised purple with the last of the sun. It sat still as a grave, shutters closed, no smoke from the chimney. The porch sagged under the weight of vines and years, and the door hung slightly ajar. An owl hooted once, then went quiet.

Gervais raised his hand, and the men stopped. All breathing hard, all trying to act like they weren't afraid of a house with no lights on.

"Maybe they're gone," Lionel muttered.

"Maybe hiding inside," said Jules, tightening his grip on his shotgun.

Gervais stepped forward first, his boots sinking into the soft ground and dead leaves. He pushed the door open with the barrel of his shotgun.

The cabin was empty.

Just dry air, curling dust, and the faint smell of herbs and smoke. A few jars on the shelf. A blanket folded at the foot of a cot. A rusted tin cup is on the table.

Someone spotted fresh footprints leading from the cabin into the darkness of the swamp.

Onionhead!

#

Sitting in the cabin, Solomon knew that they were coming for him, long before they even got close. The croaks of the frogs, the wind through the trees, and sounds tend to carry in the darkness—especially sounds that didn't belong when you are used to the sounds of nature.

He didn't wait for them. He walked off into the surrounding darkness long before they even got close, disappearing into the water and plants like a shadow.

#

The trail vanished, headed toward the bayou, swallowed up in the tangled swamp beyond. Some said he doubled back. Others said he was circling like a fox, waiting for them to leave.

They didn't care.

And silence.

Gervais stood in the doorway for a long moment. Then he turned, jaw clenched.

"Do it."

A man raised his shotgun and fired through the open window. Glass shattered, wood splintered.

Another blast followed, then another.

The porch lit up with muzzle flashes as more men joined in, riddling the cabin with buckshot. Curtains danced like ghosts in the gunfire. A shelf collapsed. Something inside caught—maybe an oil lamp—flaring for just a second before sputtering out.

No one cheered.

When it was over, they stood staring at the torn-up doorway, the sagging roof, the gaping holes in the walls.

"I don't think they were here," one of them said, wiping sweat from his brow with a trembling hand.

Gervais didn't answer. He turned and walked back into the trees, lantern swinging at his side.

Behind them, the cabin creaked once in the wind, as if letting out a tired breath.

#

Solomon heard the gunfire rolling across the dark waters and through the looming cypress. It echoed with fear and anger.

He stood at the edge of the bayou, barefoot in the mud, watching the water coil around the cypress roots. His heart ached. Mary-Ellen's death had torn something open in the town—and all that pain was curling toward him now, like smoke from a flame.

He could feel it coming.

In his mind, he saw those boys again, younger than, but just as cruel.

"Onionhead."

The word echoed like it had that first day—sharp, silly, and venomous.

But now, it meant something else. Now it was how the town saw him: not just strange, but capable of evil.

He sat down slowly in the mud, laying his hands flat on the earth like roots. The memory of his mother's voice came back, clear as wind:

"They call you that 'cause they scared. And scared people lie."

He wanted to cry. But he didn't. He hadn't in years.

Instead, he reached into his coat pocket, pulled out a small bundle wrapped in muslin: herbs for protection. He pressed it into the earth, whispered her prayer, and let the water carry the words away.

#

The next morning, some other men found Onionhead crouched by the bayou, wrapped in a muddy wool coat, shivering. He had known the men were coming last night—the frogs, trees, and wind had warned him. He walked about a mile through the woods to a place he knew. A quiet spot along the bayou where no one hardly ever came. Where he could sit at peace for a little while. He didn't say much when they brought him to town. Didn't beg. Just looked around at the broken faces and the little cross placed by the tracks and knew.

He was locked in jail *for his own protection*, though nobody said the word *protection* out loud. Marshal Kincaid brought him food and sat with him some nights. "You didn't do this," the marshal said quietly once, and Solomon only blinked, slow and tired. "I know you didn't."

But knowing and proving are different things in a town that wants a monster more than it wants the truth.

#

The morning sun came shy and pale through the dusty windows of Dumont's Feed & Provisions, filtering through burlap sacks and rows of mason jars filled with nails, sugar, and molasses.

Rosalie stood near the back counter, her hand resting lightly on a bundle of dried cornmeal. She wasn't here for cornmeal.

Behind the counter, Gervais Boudreaux rang up an older woman's purchase, grunting his usual pleasantries. He was a square-shouldered man with a pinched mouth and callused hands, his shirt sleeves always rolled up to the elbows no matter the season. He'd been quiet since the cabin incident, but then again, Gervais had always been a man of few words—unless he'd had a few drinks.

Rosalie knew.

He was one of them.

Not just by rumor, but by the way he carried himself afterward—like a man listening for distant hoofbeats. Like a man expecting judgment to come in the flesh.

"Got any more of that river cane sugar?" she asked mildly when the other customer had gone.

Gervais blinked, nodded toward a barrel by the back window. She didn't move.

Instead, Rosalie tilted her head and said, almost idly:

"You heard 'bout that doll Solomon found?"

Gervais stilled.

"Doll?"

"Mm," she said, pretending to examine her nails. "Porcelain thing. Found it just after the storm, sittin' pretty as you please on the edge of his land. The dress still had lace on it."

He said nothing.

She didn't look at him when she added:

"Funny thing. Looked just like the one that Ledoux girl used to carry 'round."

Gervais grunted. "Could'a come downriver."

"Maybe. Could'a. *"*

The air between them thickened. Somewhere outside, a mule brayed. A ceiling fan ticked in slow circles overhead.

At last, Gervais said, "You get that from him? Onionhead?"

She gave a small nod. "Stopped by to check on him after the storm. Figured you'd be glad to know he made it."

Gervais' jaw worked.

"I ain't concerned with that boy."

Rosalie smiled faintly. "Don't seem like he's concerned with you either."

She turned, picked up her parcel, and headed for the door. But just before she left, she paused beside Jules Rousseau, sitting in the corner, stringing hooks onto a cord. He looked up—red-eyed, smelling faintly of whiskey even before noon.

She leaned in, her voice soft but sharp: "Storm washed up more than water. Washed up secrets, too. And, you ruin a man's home in the dark, well... best be ready when the dark remembers."

Then she walked out.

Jules looked up at Gervais, whose mouth had gone bone white. Neither spoke.

But for the rest of the morning, they both kept glancing at the windows—as if expecting the woods to look back.

#

The bell above the door of Weller's Cobbler Shop clinked once, then again as it swayed in the wind. Jasper Weller stood behind the counter, polishing a child's boot that no one had yet claimed. The leather was cracked, the toe scuffed. It had been left outside in the rain, lost in the weeds behind the schoolhouse.

Outside, Slidell simmered. Word of the ribbon and scrap of her dress had spread like fire through dry cane. And then there was the little wooden dog. The boy had left a mark, they said. Signed it, like he wanted to be found. Men gathered tighter on porches now. They carried their anger like tools.

But Jasper couldn't stop thinking about the toys.

He reached beneath the counter and pulled out a small wooden fox. The tail curled like smoke; eyes blackened with coal ash. One of Solomon Moreau's. Left for his niece two springs ago, back when she was still coming around on Saturdays.

She never played with it, not really. She said it made her feel *"cold in her hands."* But she never threw it away, either.

Just kept it on her windowsill, like it was *watching something*.

Jasper turned the fox over in his hands, studying the weight of it. The carving was delicate, intricate. Too much patience for a child, really. It had a strange kind of grace—something wild and old beneath its smooth surface.

"He couldn't have…" he whispered aloud, shaking his head. "That boy couldn't have done that to a little girl."

But the dog. The one found under the thorn bush. That one had Solomon's mark. No denying it.

Still—

Jasper had seen the way Solomon walked: eyes on the ground, never bold enough to stare. How he always set the toys down without watching who picked them up. How he never smiled when a child liked one—but always seemed relieved.

That wasn't a killer's heart.

But the town didn't care about hearts now. It cared about signs. About answers.

The toys had once seemed like gifts.

Now they felt like breadcrumbs.

Jasper put the fox away.

He didn't know what to believe anymore.

#

The wooden dog sat on the marshal's desk, catching the slanting morning light through the shuttered window. Its chipped ear cast a bent shadow across a stack of witness statements no one had finished reading.

Andrea Vann stood across the room, arms folded tight over her chest. The cotton of her apron was dusted with flour; she'd come straight from the kitchen, halfway through kneading dough, when her son said, *"That's like the one Solomon gave me."*

That was hours ago.

She hadn't gone back.

She stared at the carving like it might twitch or speak. Like it held something she hadn't seen before.

Everyone knew his work. That was his gift. His curse. The same hands that could carve such delicate, perfect creatures had become the hands they feared.

It didn't look evil.

It didn't look like anything but small, delicate.

Innocent.

Like *him*.

She remembered the day Jacob came home with his bird. Holding it out like treasure, eyes shining. She'd scolded him then—told him not to be bothering that Moreau boy, not to take things from strange hands. But she didn't throw it away.

Something in it had stopped her.

It was too well-made. Too alive.

And she'd thought, just for a moment, *that boy can't be all bad, not with hands that do this.*

She kept the bird. Put it on the kitchen shelf beside the sugar jar. It was still there now.

But this dog...

This one had been found near the girl. Stuck in the weeds like a dropped truth.

Andrea rubbed her arms, suddenly cold despite the heat.

"Maybe he didn't mean no harm," she whispered. "Maybe he just... dropped it."

Marshal Kincaid didn't look up.

71

Or maybe he didn't want to.

He'd known Marie Moreau since before she turned gray. He'd once brought his own wife to her for tea when the baby wouldn't come. She never told. She never asked for a coin. Just handed over the cup and said, *"Drink it warm. And don't speak after."*

He didn't want to believe her boy was capable of something like this.

But the carving sat there, undeniable.

Andrea looked down at it again.

"He never looked at them right," she murmured. "Never joined in. Just stood there... starin'. Like he was somewhere else in his head."

Marshal Kincaid finally spoke, quiet.

"Or maybe we never looked at him right."

That hung in the air a long time.

Long enough for the dust to settle. Long enough for guilt to rise like heat off the floor.

Andrea didn't answer. She turned and left without saying goodbye.

The dog stayed still.

Watching.

###

9. SOLOMON GOES HOME AGAIN

The key turned in the lock with a hollow click, loud in the stillness of the jail. Morning light filtered through the barred window, casting long slats across the floor where Solomon sat, unmoving, his back against the wall.

Marshal Kincaid stood there for a moment, key still in the door, staring at the boy—no, not a boy. A young man now, though he'd never been given the chance to become one properly. Solomon's hands rested in his lap; knuckles scabbed from holding too tight to fear or prayer or whatever kept him calm.

"You can go," the marshal said, his voice more gravel than tone. "Ain't no charges."

Solomon didn't move right away. He just blinked, slowly, like the words hadn't made it all the way to his bones.

Kincaid cleared his throat. "Can't hold you no longer, son. We waited. Nothin' else came. No new tracks. No confessions. No witnesses." He rubbed the back of his neck. "Some folks still think you did it. Some always will. But the law ain't got enough to say you did."

Solomon stood. He didn't speak. He rarely did. But his eyes, wide and glass-dark, fixed on the marshal's for a long second—long enough that Kincaid had to look away.

"You go on out the back way," he muttered. "Take the pine trail. Stay off the main road."

Solomon stepped past him, light-footed and silent, like something used to moving through shadows.

Outside, the wind stirred the dust. No one waited for him. The town was quiet but not sleeping. Doors were open just a crack. Curtains moved where eyes watched.

Someone whispered, "That's him."

A little boy clutched his mother's skirt as she pulled him into the store.

Across the street, a man spat in the dirt and didn't break his stare.

Solomon walked on.

At the edge of town, a dog barked once and fell silent. The woods opened before him like an old friend—dark, indifferent, and familiar.

Back at the jail, Marshal Kincaid sat down at his desk and stared at the blotter, where no name had ever been written.

He whispered to the empty room, "God help him."

And for a moment, he wasn't sure if he meant Solomon… or the town.

#

The path twisted beneath Solomon's feet like an old scar through the woods—familiar and half-healed. The sounds of town had long since fallen away, replaced by the hush of pines and the brittle snap of the underbrush. Here, the air smelled of damp bark, sweet rot, and the faintest trace of dried sage.

When the cabin came into view, he stopped.

The porch sagged deeper now. Holes gaped in the walls like open wounds. Window frames were blackened around the edges where fire had licked but not caught. The front door hung crooked on a splintered hinge.

But smoke curled from the chimney.

A pale sheet fluttered in the breeze—clean, hung to dry.

And then he saw her.

Marie stood beside the steps, wringing out a rag over a dented basin. Her back was bent, one shoulder slightly higher than the other, a long skirt smudged with ash and pine sap. She turned her head as if she'd heard his heart before his footsteps.

Her eyes met his. Quiet. Knowing. No tears, no surprise.

Solomon moved without speaking, without thinking, across the clearing, over the crushed flowers and broken shells, up the creaking steps.

He reached her.

She opened her arms.

And he fell into them.

He buried his face against her shoulder, arms wrapped tight around her, tighter than he ever had, like he was afraid the world might rip her away too. She didn't say a word. Just held him, one hand in his hair, the other pressed firm against his back.

"You're home," she whispered, finally.

He nodded into her shoulder, throat tight. The forest stood quiet around them.

After a long moment, she pulled back and cupped his face in her work-rough hands. "Ain't much left," she said softly, glancing toward the cabin. "But I've stitched what I could. Boards. Curtains. My heart."

Solomon looked past her at the ruin, the shot-up windows, the scorched frame—but there were herbs drying on the rafters again. A kettle on the coals. A chair pulled up to the hearth.

He looked back at her. "It's enough."

Marie smiled—not wide, but deep—and led him inside.

The forest closed in behind them, cradling what was left.

###

10. BOILING POINT

There was something *wrong* in the air.

It wasn't just the heat, though it clung like wet burlap. It was the silence. The way the conversation dried up when someone entered a room. The way people crossed the street when they saw neighbors they used to call by name.

Shutters closed earlier now. Dogs barked at nothing and wouldn't be quieted. Children weren't left outside, even in daylight.

And no one went near the tracks.

Mary-Ellen's death had done something to Slidell—not just cracked it, but warped it. The town turned inward. Suspicious. Ugly. People started seeing ghosts in daylight. Shadows where none had been before. Every cough sounded like a cry. Every creak on a porch was a footstep from something wicked.

At the diner, gossip brewed faster than chicory coffee.

"I heard she was found with marks on her arms," whispered Eula, over a plate of grits gone cold. "Like hands too big for a man."

"Heard her mouth was sewn shut," muttered Derrik, not looking up.

"That ain't true," said Marshal Kincaid, overhearing from the next booth. "You know damn well—"

But no one listened to the marshal anymore. Not since he said, "We don't have a suspect yet."

To the town, that meant he wasn't going to do a damn thing.

Rumors had become more than idle talk. They were fuel.

"He's always starin'," someone said.

"Talks to himself in gibberish," added another.

"His mama doesn't even go to church," said a third. "You ever see what she's got hangin' on her porch?"

No one said Onionhead's name much, at first. They didn't need to. Everyone knew who was meant.

The Moreau had always lived on the edge—physically and morally. Marie, with her Creole roots and jars of herbs. Solomon with his twisted back, long limbs, and too-quiet eyes.

They were never **of** the town. Just **near** it. Close enough to blame.

And what started as whispers became stories. What began as doubt turned into belief.

One woman swore she saw Solomon pulling apart a bird with his bare hands.

Another claimed he walked barefoot through fire as a child. Someone said he was born from a storm, and his father was the devil himself.

The lies were outrageous, but no one laughed.

Because deep down, they needed it to be true. Needed someone to carry the weight of this horror. Someone *different enough* to deserve it.

Fear made them hungry for certainty. Grief made them violent.

And by the third day of his release, a new sound began to echo through the town—not laughter, not talk, but *the hammering of nails.*

Men building torches. Fixing old lanterns.

Sharpening knives that hadn't seen use since the last war.

Even the preacher had gone quiet.

And still, the marshal said, *"We've got no proof."*

#

A Change in the Wind

Solomon felt it before he heard it.

The swamp air had changed—charged, as if the trees were whispering warnings through their leaves. Birds had grown silent. The water moved differently. Even the cicadas pulsed with a faster rhythm, like a drumbeat in his chest.

Mama had been praying louder each night. Not to Jesus. Not in English.

She swept salt across the doorstep. Burned cedar and rue. Buried an old spoon under the porch.

"Sol," she said softly one night, "Don't go near town."

"Why?" he asked.

But he already knew. He'd seen it in the way the grocer wouldn't meet his eye. The way old Mr. Dugas clutched his daughter's hand when Solomon passed too close on the road. The way someone had painted a red X on a tree near the trail to the cabin.

He wasn't sure what it meant. Only that it wasn't good.

"They're scared, baby," Marie said. "And scared folk do stupid, wicked things."

#

79

The bell above the office door jangled sharp as a cry. Maybell stormed in with her arms wrapped around a torn piece of fabric—mud-stained, white with faded pink and red flowers. Another torn piece of Mary-Ellen's favorite dress.

"Marshal!" she hollered. "Marshal Kincaid!"

People trooped behind her to the marshal's office and now stood in the door, looking.

The marshal looked up, sweat beading his brow. "What is it?"

"I found this," she said, voice trembling, "in the woods near the Moreau trail. Caught on a bush. This is Mary-Ellen's."

He took it from her hands slowly, gently. The fabric was stiff. Something dark had dried into it.

"You're sure?" he asked.

"I stitched that hem myself," Maybell whispered, voice cracking.

Kincaid looked down at the cloth. At the dirt and the blood and the horror rising in his gut. Still, his mouth worked to form reason.

"Maybell... this doesn't prove—"

"It's his," she hissed. "Who else lives out there? Who else watches little girls from the edge of the trees? Who else never talks straight? Who else lets his mama talk to the dead?"

A murmur rippled through the crowd like wind through dry grass.

"They already buried the child," someone muttered. "And still nothin's been done."

"What's the marshal waitin' for? A signed confession?"

"She was five years old."

Someone spat. Another wept openly.

#

Earl Stagg stood on his porch with a shotgun across his knees and a jug of rye near his boot heel. The sky was turning that strange burnt-red of an evening thick with heat and mosquitoes. Train whistles moaned in the distance—low, sorrowful, like a warning the land had already stopped listening to.

He still had trouble sleeping.

Ever since they found Mary-Ellen on the tracks.

That little girl had played hopscotch with his own granddaughter. Had stolen peaches from his yard and run off giggling like a bandit. She used to call him "Old Bear," the way she did all the men who gave her candy and let her tug their beards.

Now she was *gone*. Torn. Left like trash beside the rails.

And something in Earl had cracked.

Logic didn't live in him anymore. Just the image of that body, that lost doll, and the goddamn dog in the thicket.

That carved thing. Pretty, yes—but made by *that boy*. That *thing*.

He remembered when the Moreau boy—*Onionhead!*— came around the feed store years ago. Quiet as ever. Standing behind his mama, who smelled like herbs and smoke and something else no one could name. Marie Moreau. A woman

81

who looked right through you. Who never smiled, not really. Just stared, like she knew something about you that you didn't want said out loud.

He'd never trusted her.

Never trusted the boy either. That face and off-shaped head. That silence. Those toys.

Earl remembered the fox his grandson had brought home once. Beautiful little thing. Sharp ears, tail curled like a question mark. But his dog wouldn't go near it. Barked until the fox was thrown in the bayou. That should've been a warning enough.

He took a swig from the jug and wiped his mouth.

They were saying a crowd was gathering soon. Going out toward the Moreau cabin. Folks wanted answers. Some wanted blood.

Earl wanted both.

The way he saw it, if they didn't stop this now, there'd be another child gone. Another mother screaming down by the tracks. Another toy left like a signature.

"Boy's not right," he muttered to the dark.

And he believed it.

Not because of evidence. Not because of what made sense.

But because *he had to*.

Because grief needed an outlet.

And hate always found its shape.

#

The Mob Forms

It started on the church steps.

Not with fire and shouting, but with quiet voices and sideways glances—grief curdling into suspicion. The kind of talk that begins with hushed tones and ends with ruined lives.

It was Sunday morning, and the bell of St. Jude's had just finished ringing over the town, marking the end of services. The townsfolk filed out slowly, fanning themselves beneath the already sweltering sky. The women clutched lace handkerchiefs and whispered behind gloved hands. The men stood in loose, sweaty circles, sleeves rolled, tobacco burning at their lips.

And no one was talking about the sermon.

They were talking about Mary-Ellen Ledoux.

Her death still hung over Slidell like a thundercloud, thick with pressure. It had been a week since her body was found—torn, bruised, curled up beside the railroad tracks like something tossed away. Her mother hadn't left her room since. Her father hadn't been sober.

And no one knew whose fault it was—not really.

Yet, everyone knew who was to blame.

"He was seen near the edge of town a few days before," said Frank Gautreaux, eyes narrow beneath his straw hat. "Just standin' there by the tracks. Starin'."

"That boy was always starin'," muttered Gervais Boudreaux, chewing the end of a matchstick. "Ain't never right in the head. You seen it."

"God don't twist a man up like that for no reason," said Missy Foret, voice low and wary.

"That ain't a man," someone else added. "That's a mistake hidin' in a skin."

The words passed from mouth to mouth like an infection.

Solomon Moreau— *"Onionhead"* —the deformed boy who lived in the swamp, the son of a woman some called a healer and others called a witch.

They said he never spoke unless he had to.

That he fed raccoons like pets.

That he left strange herbs wrapped in palm leaves on people's porches when their babies were sick.

#

At first, they'd pitied him.

Then they feared him.

Now, they were ready to hate.

"I say we go out there," Gervais said. "We go out tonight. Ask questions. Make him talk. If he won't—"

"Then we make sure he can't hurt nobody else," Jules finished.

There was a pause.

The men looked at each other—guiltless and grim.

No one said the word lynch.

No one had to.

They just nodded.

That night, when the moon was thin and sickle-shaped, they gathered behind the old grain mill. No one brought rope—they didn't need it.

The women stayed home, silent and complicit, watching lamps flickering in their windows. All except Maybell Allemond. She helped raise little Mary-Ellen, and her anger had turned into a roaring fury that could only be quenched by blood. She wouldn't be left behind—she had to be there.

And not one of them thought to ask whether Solomon had ever truly laid a hand on the child.

Because it wasn't the justice they wanted.

It was certainty.

And certainty came easier than truth.

###

11. TORCHES IN THE DARK

Rosalie knew something was wrong the moment she saw the torches and lanterns.

They bobbed behind the old grain mill, low and tight to the ground—held by men hunched in the dark like conspirators, not neighbors. Ten of them, maybe twelve. All familiar. All dangerous when grief outweighed sense.

She stepped off the road and walked straight toward them.

The night smelled of kerosene and heat. Crickets stopped singing as she passed.

"Jules," she said, voice sharp but calm. "I know what y'all are planning."

The men froze like boys caught with matches. Gervais Boudreaux turned, his face flickering gold in the lantern light.

"Rosalie, this ain't none of your concern."

"You make it mine the moment you start takin' justice into your own hands." She looked around at the others—Frank Gautreaux, Lionel Cormier, Billy Simms, Earl Staggs, and others. Even Maybell Allemond, the only woman in the group and one with the most fire in her eyes, like a crazed cat ready to scrap. All with stiff mouths and sweating brows. All holding something they hadn't earned: certainty.

"Y'all think you're righteous," she said. "But what if you're wrong?"

Frank spat into the grass. "That thing ain't right. He's always skulkin' around. Never speaks. Can't even look you in the eye. Who else coulda done it?"

Rosalie stepped closer. Her voice dropped.

"Fear don't make truth, Frank. Just makes smoke."

Jules's hand tightened on the handle of an axe. "You didn't see that poor child. The state she was in."

"I did," Rosalie said. "And I also saw the doll Solomon found after the storm. Her doll. It washed up at his door, just like the day she went missin'. You ever know a flood to return what the river takes?"

That made them pause.

But not long enough.

"Witchcraft, then," someone muttered. "His mama is one. You know it."

"Marie is a healer," Rosalie snapped. "Y'all lined up for her tonics soon as your lungs started wheezin'. Funny how folk love a woman's work until they need someone to blame."

Silence. The kind that meant her words had struck bone.

She looked Jules in the eye.

"You burn that boy's home tonight, you ain't makin' the town safe. You're just lettin' your grief turn to hate. And hate'll eat what's left of your soul before the fire even catches."

Jules looked down at the can in his hands.

Frank wouldn't meet her eyes.

For a second, the tension broke. For just a moment, she thought she'd reached them.

But then Billy muttered, "Maybe she's in on it too."

That was all it took.

The flicker of doubt turned into heat again. Gervais pushed past her, his mouth tight.

"We're done talkin', Rosalie."

Lanterns bobbed. Boots scraped gravel. The men moved off into the trees.

She stood there, fists clenched, watching them vanish like phantoms into the dark.

And above the grain mill, the clouds began to gather again—heavy, low, as if the sky itself was holding its breath.

#

Inside the cabin, lit by the faint orange glow of a single oil lamp, Marie moved in slow, practiced circles. She placed dried herbs in the fire—angelica, cedar, and dried snakeskin. The smell filled the room like a forgotten memory.

She spoke, not in English, but in the tongue her grandmother had whispered through closed doors. *Patwa*, old Creole French with words older still. Words that weren't written anywhere. Words the land still knew.

Solomon sat cross-legged on the floor, head bowed.

"You feel it, baby?" she said, voice like a spell.

He nodded.

"They're comin'. Maybe tonight. Maybe tomorrow. But they got it in their heads now. Their fears turned to poison."

"I didn't hurt her," Solomon said. His voice was quiet, steady. "I'd never hurt her."

"You don't have to convince me, bébé," Marie said. She leaned in, pressing her fingers—warm and dry—to his temples.

"The truth ain't what keeps a mob back. Fear keeps a mob back. Or blood."

She picked up an old bone talisman from the hearth and held it to the light. It had been carved long ago—etched with crooked lines no man could read.

"Don't speak, not a word," she said in the old tongue. "When they come, you run. Like shadow, like fox, like breath."

Outside, thunder grumbled from far off in the swamp.

And in the woods, something shifted—like trees remembering their roots.

#

The wind had shifted.

It came down from the cypress trees now, low and thick, as if it carried messages from the old world. The kind spoken without lips. The kind that reached only those who remembered.

Marie Moreau lit a small candle in a blue glass jar and placed it in the window.

The flame didn't flicker.

She whispered words as she crushed dried leaves in her palm—verveine, menthe, and anis. Not spells, she'd say, if asked. Just things her grandmother taught her. Things meant to keep illness away. To protect a home from gossip. To ward off sorrow.

But people in Slidell didn't believe in herbs. They believed in whispers.

And they whispered plenty about Marie.

Some said she was a *traiteuse*, a healer. Others said she was a witch. Others still said she'd once called lightning down with a cry.

What the truth was, no one could say. Not even Solomon.

To him, she was just Mama. But sometimes—even he felt it.

Felt the stillness in the cabin after she spoke the old words. The way fire bent slightly toward her fingers. The way crows gathered near her garden but never picked a single fruit.

Tonight, she walked barefoot across the floorboards, murmuring under her breath. She took a jar of white powder—eggshells, ground fine—and blew it across the threshold. The dust scattered like snow, like ash. Like a line in the sand.

Then she sat beside the hearth and sang—not loudly, not in tune. Just a low, cracked melody in a language no book had ever held. The kind of tune that had no start, no end. Just the steady rhythm of dirt and bones and memory.

Solomon watched her from his cot, knees drawn up. He wanted to ask what the words meant. But he didn't. Not tonight.

"Mama," he said instead, "What if they don't listen?"

Marie didn't look at him right away. Just kept stirring the air with her words.

"They won't," she said finally.

"Then why—"

"Because if I don't speak 'em," she said, voice dry as tinder, "then who else will?"

#

90

Outside, the trees swayed.

Something creaked in the woods.

She looked up toward the window, toward the candle flame—still standing straight as a soldier.

"They're coming," she said quietly.

And then, switching to that old tongue again, she muttered something soft, barely a breath:

"Pas touche mon fils. Laissez les morts prendre les vivants."

(Do not touch my son. Let the dead take the living.)

Was it a prayer? A threat? A lullaby?

Solomon didn't ask. He just closed his eyes.

And somewhere deep in the swamp, a bullfrog stopped croaking. The trees stood still. And the candle flickered once.

Just once.

###

12. THEY COME FOR HIM

The woods were hot and close. The cicadas screamed. A dirt path led up to a crooked shack half-swallowed by Spanish moss and wild vines.

The heat was thick enough to drink, and the woods pressed in close like eavesdroppers. Eleven figures trudged up the dirt path, their boots caked in mud and spite. At their front, a rangy hound—black and low to the ground—sniffed the air and let out a low growl. Its handler, a wiry man named Burl, held the leash tight. They came armed with rifles, clubs, and rusted tools. They came not for answers—but for vengeance.

Ahead, the crooked silhouette of the Moreau cabin emerged from the trees like a twisted bone sticking out of the earth. The paint had long peeled away. There were holes here and there, and all the windows were broken. The porch sagged like a mouth missing teeth. From within: no sound. No movement.

The group gathered at the edge of the clearing, breathing hard. Covered in muck. Stinking of sweat and righteousness. And still… no one stepped forward.

Smoke curled from the chimney—faint, earthy.

They stopped. Not because they were tired, but because **this** was the edge.

Until Lyle Wesson, the youngest, twenty and trembling, muttered, "What if they're waitin' inside? What if he's watchin' us right now?"

"There it is," Jules grunted, pointing with his axe to the sagging shack ahead. "Keep your eyes peeled. The freak's close."

Then—at the edge of the woods behind the cabin—a flash of motion. A bent figure burst from the back of 'the shack and disappeared into the trees.

"There he goes!" someone shouted.

"It's him!"

"Solomon! You coward! Get back here!"

They gave chase for half a breath, but the brambles were thick and the swamp hungry. The man—Onionhead, as they cruelly called him—was gone, swallowed by shadow.

"Dammit," muttered Jules, clutching the axe he'd brought from his shed. "Slippery freak's faster than he looks."

"Then we take it out on what's left," spat Maybell, her eyes wild.

The mob turned back toward the cabin.

#

The front door creaked open with a slow, aching sound. From within stepped Marie Moreau. She stood tall despite her age, eyes gleaming like wet coal. Her long skirt brushed the porch floor; her hair coiled in silver-black ropes. In one hand, a bundle of dried herbs; in the other, a bone-handled knife, held with purpose.

She looked at them like a mother bear cornered by wolves.

"Don't you hurt a hair on my baby boy's head," she said, voice low but cutting through the heat like a blade. "I swear by all the gods I know, if you do, you'll regret it 'til your dying breath."

Gervais didn't flinch. *"He ran. Only the guilty run."*

"He ain't done no wrong." She snapped. "You think that makes him guilty? You ain't come for truth. You come for blood."

"He's hiding something," Gervais barked. "Maybe it's time somebody made that boy answer for what he's done."

"He's a monster!" Maybell screamed. "You think we don't know what he did?"

Marie stepped forward, just one step. The porch boards groaned beneath her bare feet.

"Y'all don't know nothing," she hissed. "You hear a lie enough times and start wearing it like gospel. But I see the truth clearer than you ever will."

"Where is he, Marie?" another man growled.

She lifted her chin. "Where you can't reach him."

The wind shifted. The air grew suddenly thick, as if the trees themselves were holding their breath.

"You listen close now," she said, her voice dropping to a near whisper. "If you harm my boy... if one of you so much as lays a wicked hand on him... you'll carry that weight to your grave. Each and every one of you. You'll be cursed for life. Your crops will rot, your babes will be stillborn, and you'll hear him howling in your dreams 'til the day you die."

For a moment, the forest held its breath.

There was silence. Not even the cicadas dared make a sound.

The dog whimpered, tail drooping. The air shifted.

#

Some in the mob faltered—shuffling their feet, avoiding her gaze. Maybell crossed herself behind her back. Only Gervais stood firm.

But Gervais gritted his teeth and spat in the dirt.

"I ain't afraid of your curses," he said. "I'm afraid of letting a monster run free while a little girl was buried way too young. If you won't give him up, then we'll find him ourselves."

"They ain't meant to scare you," she said. "They're meant to warn you."

"Go on then," Marie growled. "Let the dog lead you straight into Hell."

Marie's eyes narrowed.

She looked at each man in turn.

"You ain't here for justice," she said. "You're here for comfort. You want somethin' to bleed for what you lost. But my boy ain't your answer."

Then she raised her free hand—her thumb sliced across her palm, blood dripped onto the porch steps—and chanted something low and old, something that had no English in it. The air seemed to twist. A crow shrieked overhead.

The mob stumbled back.

"Go on, then," she said, pointing the blade toward them. "Burn the house if you're feeling brave. But when your fields fail and your children cry out in their sleep... you'll remember tonight."

They didn't stay long after that. One by one, the fire drained from their eyes, and they turned back toward town. Muttering. Muttering—but leaving.

And in the trees, deep in the shadows, Onionhead watched. Watched as his mama stood alone on that porch like a fortress.

Watched and wept in silence.

\#

Burl pulled the dog's leash, and the hound growled, sniffed, and pulled toward the dark trees. The hound barked furiously, surging against its leash.

"Get that dog on the trail!" Gervais shouted.

Burl knelt, showed the dog a piece of worn cloth taken from the Moreau laundry line. The hound whined, caught the scent, and with a low growl, began pulling them toward the woods.

Marie stood alone on the porch as they disappeared into the trees, her fingers trembling but her gaze steady. She watched them until the last back vanished between the trunks, then slowly raised the sachet to her lips and blew the dust into the wind.

"Si vous le touchez, vous porterez la malédiction jusqu'à la tombe!"

(If you hurt him, you'll carry the curse to your grave.)

The wind carried it eastward—toward the chasing crowd.

And deep in the swamp, Onionhead was running. Through thorn and muck, where no man dared tread. But behind him, the hound howled, and the hunt had begun.

\#

Into the swamp

The dog strained at the leash, nose low, tail stiff, dragging Burl through a narrow break in the trees. The others followed, single file at first, then bunched and staggered, jostling through tangled underbrush and groping vines that seemed to grab at their ankles like ghost hands.

The woods swallowed them quickly.

What had been a path turned into a game trail, then into nothing at all—just a wild tangle of wet earth, clawing branches, and slow, stinking water. Spanish moss hung low like curtains in a haunted house, brushing against their faces with each step. The sky and moon above became a memory, choked out by the canopy above. The air itself thickened—soupy, buzzing with mosquitoes, gnats, and biting flies that clung to skin and hair.

Gervais cursed as his boot sank deep into black mud, coming up with a sick squelch and half a shoe. "Goddamn this place."

"Where the hell did he go?" Maybell growled, wiping sweat from her brow, which had already smeared her rouge into red streaks.

"Dog's got the scent," Burl grunted, yanking the hound onward, though it too moved slower now—whining, its paws pulling free of muck with effort. "Keep moving."

They did—but it was not easy. Every step came at a price. A root snagged a shin. A branch snapped back into someone's face. A hornet's nest hidden in a hollow log sent three of them running in a panic, swatting their necks and ears. One man fell knee-deep into a still pool, screaming at the squirm of something unseen beneath the surface. Another stopped to wrench a thorn from his calf, blood seeping through his pant leg.

And yet, despite all this, Solomon— "Onionhead" —was nowhere in sight.

Once, Billy caught a glimpse: a fleeting figure darting through the cypress, his thin arms cutting through brush like wings, his bare feet silent on the spongy ground. There was no trail, no crash of branches—just motion, fast and sure. He moved like a rabbit through a briar patch, vanishing before they could shout his name.

"He knows this place," someone muttered. "Like he was born in it."

"He was," Lionel's warning echoed in Gervais's head, but he shook it off like a fly.

"Keep moving!"

The swamp grew worse.

#

It had already taken hours to push through the mud and thicket. The woods weren't kind. Vines tugged at ankles like fingers from the grave. Mosquitoes hummed around ears and eyes. A cottonmouth slid through brush—angry at their intrusion—sending three men jumping and swearing.

The hound—old Duke, normally good-nosed and silent, had gone strange about a mile back. He'd whined and pulled and finally planted his legs, refusing to go further. Burl shouted, jerking at the rope tied to the dog. Reluctantly, the dog started forward along the trail again. This time, it didn't pull at the rope, trying to follow the trail. It moved slow at first—hesitant—then a little quicker, still taking cautious steps as it moved ahead.

And still, they pressed on.

Eleven people. Sweat-soaked. Half of them are limping. All of them are afraid to say it out loud.

They were close now. They could feel it.

"They knew we were comin'," someone said, thinking back to the cabin.

"Goddamn witch," someone else muttered. "She's got that devil sense."

"Enough," Gervais said, voice tight. "She was just talkin' nonsense."

#

Midnight found the swamp hushed and breathless. Even the crickets held their tongues.

The group moved in a crooked line, torches and lanterns bobbing through the brush like ghost-lights. Jules led, his axe slung over his shoulder. Gervais followed silently, eyes fixed ahead. Earl Staggs hobbled behind them, gripping his walking stick in one hand and a flask in the other. Lionel Cormier trailed last, sweating despite the night chill, fingers white around the worn handle of an old sugarcane knife. Lionel's hand shook.

They had to pass through a narrow stretch where the water rose to their thighs, murky and reeking, filled with floating things best left unnamed. Cypress knees jutted from the water like drowned fingers. Maybell, slipping, reached for a trunk and recoiled when a fat green snake slid away just beneath the bark.

The air buzzed louder. The humid air pressed harder. Time stopped making sense.

And still, Onionhead stayed just ahead—always ahead.

He wasn't running blindly. He was guiding himself by memory, by instinct. While they hacked and stumbled, he slipped through hidden hollows and narrow deer paths known only to the swamp's children. This was his world. They didn't belong here. And the swamp knew it.

One by one, the mob began to fray—panting, red-faced, covered in sweat and welts, growing slower with each step. Gervais refused to stop, but the fear had begun to creep in: not of Solomon, but of something deeper. Something older.

Because deep in the heart of the bayou, the trees leaned closer. The wind whispered names no one remembered teaching it. The swamp had taken many things over the years—bodies, secrets, time—and it didn't like to give anything back.

Least of all vengeance.

#

Solomon's legs moved on instinct now, guided not by sight but by some old memory of the land—the way his mama taught him to feel for higher ground with his soles, to read the wind by how it tugged at the moss. The torchlights had fallen behind. The shouts were fainter now, though still chasing like dogs on the scent. Even the dog seemed to be quieter, forgoing the loud baying, only letting out a few random barks.

He pressed into the murk, where the cypress grew too thick for even the sun to touch and the air turned cool in a way that didn't match the season.

Something in the silence changed.

The frogs stopped croaking.

The wind stopped breathing.

The moss hung motionless, like a curtain before a stage.

And Solomon knew where he was now.

The drowned grove.

A place his mama said to avoid after nightfall—not out of fear, but out of respect. It was where the swamp forgot time. Trees stood warped and leaning like penitents. The water was as still as black glass. No paths. No signs. Just the hum of something old and watching.

He stepped carefully, his breath clouding even in the humid dark.

Then—a *sound*.

Not a voice exactly, but close. Like someone whispering underwater.

"Solomon..." —like a whisper in the wind, but there was no wind. Only stillness.

He froze.

Turned. Nothing behind him but vines.

"On'yunhead..."

This time, the word was clear, though it came from nowhere. Not mocking. Not cruel. Just *said*. The way a name is said when it is being... remembered.

He should have run.

But instead, Solomon stepped forward.

There was a pool—round, motionless, rimmed in driftwood and stones shaped like vertebrae. At the center of it floated a single porcelain shoe, no larger than a child's thumb. Pale blue. Glowing faintly.

His breath hitched.

There was a doll!

It matched the doll. The one from the flood. The one he'd found days ago, dry as bone and sitting on the shore like it had been waiting for him.

Then, from behind a veil of vines, a figure moved.

He saw only its outline: a woman, standing in the water, half-shrouded in hanging moss. Her skin gleamed pale. Her hair trailed behind her like roots. She wasn't standing on anything— just *there*, as if the water held her up.

Solomon didn't breathe.

She raised a finger to her lips.

Then she turned and vanished between the trees, not so much walking as slipping out of reality, the way dreams do when you wake up too fast.

A few heartbeats later, the torchlight returned—flickering far off through the trees. The men were gaining again. But Solomon didn't run.

Not yet.

Because something had changed.

He wasn't alone out here.

Not really.

And the swamp... the swamp hadn't forgotten him.

Not him,

or her.

#

The swamp was thick with breath and fury. Behind Solomon, boots crashed through mud, men huffing and rumbling, branches snapped like bones. The hunt had grown wild, confused. Some shouted his name like a curse, others, like a prayer. The dog yelped, there was a splash, then another louder splash followed by angry shouts.

His lungs burned, his feet cut on hidden roots. But still he ran—always forward, deeper into the marrow of the land.

Then, just as the brush thickened and the water began to slosh cold around his ankles, Solomon saw it.

A faint light.

Small, trembling.

Hovering low by the ground, just to his left.

Not a lantern. No flame had that color. It was bluish-white, like moonlight caught in a bottle, and it moved—not with wind, but with intent. It pulsed once, then drifted into the shadows between two knotted trees.

Solomon paused for only a moment.

Behind him, voices called out, closer now.

The light led him to high ground. A patch of dry leaves under a leaning oak where the moss hung like tattered curtains. And just like that, it was gone.

Solomon fell to his knees, panting, blinking into the silence.

#

The moment stirred something deep. A scent. A sound. A memory worn thin with time but not forgotten.

He had been small then. Maybe five. Lost. Separated from Marie in the storm after venturing too far to chase a frog.

Rain had swallowed the world. Thunder cracked the sky in half.

He had cried—loud at first, then softer, ashamed. The trees seemed enormous, dripping with hunger. He remembered calling her name—over and over.

And then—light.

Tiny. Floating.

Just like tonight.

It had drifted ahead of him slowly, pausing every few feet as if waiting. He'd followed without thinking, without doubting.

That light had led him home.

His mother had stood in the doorway of the cabin, soaked through and shaking, her eyes like fire and tears. She'd grabbed him, crushed him to her chest, whispering Creole words he didn't yet understand.

When she asked how he found his way back, he only said, "The light showed me."

She had gone still for a long moment.

Then whispered something to the trees.

#

Back in the present, Solomon touched the ground beneath him.

Cool. Solid.

Safe… for now.

Somewhere in the distance, the men were arguing. The dog was quiet. The swamp had changed its tune.

And Solomon, mud-streaked and wild-eyed, whispered a word—not English—and looked once to the trees.

There was no light now.

But he knew it had been there.

#

They'd been walking for what felt like hours—though no one could say how long for sure. The swamp had no clocks, only the heavy, unchanging weight of heat and rot. Moonlight filtered through the treetops in thin green ribbons, dancing across standing pools and mossy trunks. It was beautiful in the way a snake is beautiful, just before it strikes.

The hound still moved forward, but slower now, tongue lolling, eyes uneasy. It whined at every fork in the brush, hesitant, like even it knew they were going too far.

And then came the first voice of dissent.

"I say we turn back," muttered Harlan Dupré, his voice barely above the buzz of gnats. He was sweating through his shirt, blood crusted on his shin from a saw palmetto cut. "Ain't no sense in goin' further. This boy's gone. He's long gone."

Gervais turned on him fast, eyes sharp and furious. "You gonna quit now? When we're this close?"

"Close to what?" Harlan snapped. "We ain't seen him in over an hour. This damn swamp twists you around. We keep goin', we might not find our way out."

"He's right," said Earl Staggs, wiping at a welt swelling on his neck. "This place ain't natural. I feel watched. My knees are shakin'. I ain't ashamed to say it."

"We didn't come this far to get scared off by bugs and mud," growled Maybell. "That freak did something to that little girl. He's guilty. You want him to do it again?"

Harlan looked at her. "You saw him do it?"

Maybell opened her mouth, hesitated.

"No," she admitted sheepishly. *"But look at him. That's enough."*

More silence. A few glances exchanged. The bloodlust was cooling in some—but not all. And that was the danger.

"It's too late to go back," Gervais barked. "You heard Marie. She wants us gone, and that means her boy's guilty. Hell, he ran, didn't he? That tells me all I need to know."

"But what if she was telling the truth?" Lyle Wesson whispered. "About the curse. About what'd happen if we—"

Gervias laughed, too loudly. "You afraid of stories now? Of swamp ghosts and root charms? That old woman's been feeding people swamp weed for decades. She's half-crazy."

But Lyle didn't smile. Nor did Harlan.

And others—like Billy and Frank—were slowing down too, dragging their feet, eyes scanning the trees like they expected something to step out from behind them. Their hate had cooled into dread. But they didn't speak up. The momentum was too strong. The pack still burned with purpose, and in the heat of the mob, no one wanted to be the one to blink.

So, they kept going.

Not because they believed Solomon was guilty.

Not because they weren't afraid.

But because they didn't know how to stop.

To turn back now would be to admit they'd followed anger instead of truth. That they'd let themselves be swept up in something uglier than justice.

So, they marched on, deeper into the swamp, through hanging moss and clouds of insects, stepping over bones half-sunk in mud, past trees carved with strange markings, following a dog who didn't want to go forward either.

And above them, somewhere unseen, the crows began to circle.

#

The ground had changed again. Drier in patches, soft in others, giving way without warning to sudden sloughs of black water that stank like rot and copper. Cypress knees jutted up like gravestones, and the path the hound followed had narrowed to something that was no longer meant for men. Thornbushes tangled the edges. Vine-twined limbs hung low, demanding submission to pass beneath.

Frank wiped at his neck, now swollen from stings. His boots squelched with every step, the sole of one nearly torn off. His legs ached. His hands trembled.

"I can't keep goin' like this," he muttered, mostly to himself.

"Then fall behind," Maybell spat, not looking back. "The rest of us got a job to finish."

She still walked with fire in her limbs. Her dress was torn, her stockings shredded by thorns, but her eyes—her eyes burned. They hadn't stopped burning since little Mary-Ellen had gone missing. She was only five years old. She used to pick flowers outside the church while her mother sang in the choir.

Maybell had helped raise her.

"She was just a little girl," Maybell growled, shoving past a palmetto. "And that thing you all keep callin' 'Solomon'—that Onionhead freak—he was always watchin' her. Always skulkin' around. You think I didn't see it?"

Frank hesitated. "We don't know it was him."

Frank flinched under her glare. Her grief was a live wire, and she wrapped herself in it like armor.

But something deeper stirred in Frank now—something rawer than fear. Shame.

Levi had known Solomon since the boy was small. Had seen him pull wounded birds from the brush and try to stitch them up with his crooked hands. Solomon never talked much, never raised a hand, never raised his voice. He was strange, sure. Ugly, yes. But dangerous? Levi wasn't so sure anymore.

"I just think we're goin' too far," Lionel said quietly.

"You think that boy's gonna come back and confess? You think he'll stand trial?" Maybell laughed, harsh and joyless. "There ain't no law out here but us."

Frank and Levi looked around at the faces in the group—faces smeared with mud, insect-bitten, twisted with fatigue and fury. They didn't like what they saw.

#

"Why?"

He moved like a breath through tall grass. His limbs ached—he'd gashed his foot on a root hours ago, and the blood was sticky between his toes—but he kept going, silent as fog, faster than the dog.

He knew these woods like his own skin.

They weren't just shelter. They were memories. They were protection. His mama used to say the trees could *see* if you treated them right. That the swamp would hide you if it loved you.

And it loved Solomon.

As he ran, he listened—not just to the shouts behind him, but to the *silence* between them. The pauses when the swamp made them stop and look around. When it tricked their sense of direction. When it made them doubt each other.

He knew they hated him.

Not for anything he'd done—but for what he looked like. For what he reminded them of. Something broken. Something not quite human. He'd seen it in their eyes since he was a child.

But he wasn't going to die in this swamp. Not today.

He crouched behind a curtain of moss, letting their voices pass by—a short distance away—like angry bees. His breath came shallow, but he didn't cry. Not anymore.

He thought of Mama's voice, soft and sharp like a fiddle bow:

"You run, baby. And when the swamp sings to you, you listen. It's always sung for our kind."

And somewhere in the distance, a crow called once—then again.

Warning.

Marking time.

Solomon moved on, deeper into the place where the land remembered what the town tried to forget.

#

The night had grown quiet again—too quiet.

Even the swamp held its breath.

Solomon lay curled in a shallow ditch near the edge of some dry land, covered in vines and muck, body trembling with exhaustion. He had run as far as his legs would carry him, farther than most men could. But now, the limits had found him.

His swollen eye barely opened. Blood crusted his lip where a branch had caught him. His breath was thin and rattling.

Above him, the stars blinked through cypress limbs like distant watchers.

For a moment, he thought the mob had turned back.

Then he heard the rustle of grass.

Footsteps.

Heavy. Many.

He didn't lift his head.

The light hit his face first—lantern glow flaring golden against his pale skin, casting long shadows across the ditch.

"There he is!"

The voice came flat, more tired than triumphant. Gervais Boudreaux.

Jules stepped down into the ditch, boots squishing.

Solomon raised a hand, feeble.

"Why…" he rasped, the word ragged, barely a sound at all. So soft, it was likely no one actually heard.

They paused.

Then they dragged Solomon from the ditch like something unclean, like a sack of rags soaked in rain. He moaned once—a thin, human sound that froze even Gervais Boudreaux for a breath. But by then, mercy had already drained from them, replaced by something older.

Something superstitious.

They kicked him first. Then fists. Then sticks and stones. No real weapons—just hands and rage, like beasts tearing at meat. It started with a few. Then others joined in.

By the time the last breath left Solomon's lungs, his face was unrecognizable, the name *Onionhead* irrelevant now. His body was silent, broken open like a question no one wanted to answer. Then came the overwhelming stillness.

#

Rage Fades, Superstition Remains

Still, it wasn't enough.

Someone—maybe Levon—said, "He ain't safe, even in death. You heard what she was. You heard what they both are."

"He can't stay whole."

"If he's like her—if he's touched—he'll come back."

They looked at each other, sweaty and pale in the torchlight. Nods passed between them. Because deep down, they'd all heard the same whispers. How witches couldn't die normal deaths. How you had to divide the body, or the spirit stayed angry. Thirteen pieces. One for each apostle. One for the devil.

111

No one spoke.

They simply worked.

Knives came out—not for defense, but for ritual. Old whispers of what should be done to the body of someone touched by darkness. The heart, removed. The hands, buried apart. The tongue, cut out and burned in a flame.

They cut Solomon into thirteen parts, counting them aloud in hoarse whispers: arms, legs, hands, feet, heart, tongue, eyes, head, and torso—until all that remained was a bundle of unrecognizable flesh.

It wasn't justice. It wasn't even hatred anymore.

It was superstition wrapped in flesh.

They carried the pieces in burlap sacks, walking through the swamp in silence. The dog stayed behind, whining.

\#

The Scattered Bones

They crept into Saint Margaret's Cemetery—a short distance north of town—just before dawn, like grave robbers, avoiding the cemetery lanterns and grave stones. One by one, they buried the pieces across the grounds, as far from each other as the shadows allowed.

One beneath the crumbling angel whose face had weathered smooth.

One inside the hollow of the old hanging tree, stuffed in like a secret.

One beneath the stone cross, where children left toys for lost siblings.

One in the chapel's shade, where mold clung to the bricks like rot.

One behind the mausoleum no one visited anymore.

One beneath the fence line.

One beneath the leaning oak where no one placed flowers.

One under the broken statue of the Virgin with no hands.

And the rest - just scattered and random, mixed with soil and silence.

No grave markers.

No prayers.

Thirteen shallow graves.

Thirteen dark silences.

Just dirt, and men who would go home with red under their fingernails and no words for their wives. One by one, they left the cemetery, boots dragging, eyes low. *Only Lionel's hands and blade were blood-free—unlike his memories.*

One by one, they left the cemetery, boots dragging, eyes low.

And behind them, the wind began to move again.

It passed through the gates and over the headstones. It touched each of the burial sites with cold fingers, and somewhere, in the hush between breath and dawn, the ground seemed to shift, ever so slightly, as if something beneath had stirred.

Somewhere far off in the dark, a soft wind moved through the swamp, and the trees whispered a name—

"On'yunhead…"

#

None of them would speak of that night.

But the earth remembered.

And so did the pieces.

###

13. INNOCENCE REVEALED

The news came the very next day with the train.

Old Harvey Dupré read it off a folded newspaper at the feed store, voice cracking like the paper itself:

*"**Man Arrested in Baton Rouge… Girl's Locket Found… Confession Extracted.**"*

That was how they said it—clean, plain, and final. Just words, typed and printed and handed out like grain.

The killer's name wasn't Solomon Moreau. It was someone else. A stranger. A monster who drifted through and vanished, like a storm cloud with knives inside.

A man arrested three parishes over—passing through Alexandria—had confessed to the murder of a child. Marshal Kincaid rode out and returned with a confession written in a shaking hand. The man was a transient, a war-haunted stranger. No one from Slidell. No one, Solomon or anyone else in town, had ever met.

The people of the town never spoke his name again—not Onionhead—not Solomon. But the guilt hung there, in the creak of the church pews, in the quiet side glances, in the way children were taught to be kind to strangers—but only just so kind.

And by the tracks, beneath the pine shadow, Mary-Ellen's cross still stands. But nearby now, half-hidden in ivy and moss, is a second marker. A piece of gnarled wood, bent and crooked, and weathered by rain. If you squinted a bit, it could almost have been a twisted cross.

#

Lionel sat on the porch of his uncle's shop, boots on the rail, coffee going cold in his hand. He listened to the words float down the dusty street, watched heads nod and shoulders rise and fall with sudden relief.

"Solomon was no killer," someone said.

"No, sir. Always said it felt wrong."

"Lies. All of it."

Lionel could still smell the swamp on his coat, still see the glow of the lanterns and torches throwing shadows across the remains of Onionhead like the darkness was trying to claim what was left.

He'd watched Onionhead, beaten and brutalized without shouting, without fighting—just taking what punishment was dealt out. And all that time, he hadn't said a word. Not then. Well, maybe one. Lionel couldn't be sure if he heard it or imagined it.

"*Why?*' he had

whispered.

Only Lionel seemed the have heard anything. It came soft like a whisper carried away in the wind.

Just *why?*

At the time, Lionel didn't have any real answer.

And now it was too late.

#

Up before sunrise, Lionel walked back to the edge of the woods. Not all the way in—he didn't have that kind of courage— but far enough to see how peaceful and serene it could be at this pre-dawn hour of the morning.

116

He knelt and ran a hand through the dirt.

It wasn't just Onionhead they murdered.

It was something Lionel couldn't name, couldn't fix—some part of his soul he'd traded for a place among men who didn't know how to be good.

He looked up at the moon.

"I didn't mean for it to go that far," he whispered. "I didn't…"

His voice cracked and stopped.

He didn't cry. Not really. Just sat there while the wind pulled at his shirt, the trees rustled secrets overhead, and the world moved on without asking his permission.

Somewhere out there, the spirit of Onionhead remained in the swamp. Or maybe not. Maybe it was just the chill of the night that seemed to follow him ever since. Or loneliness in his own thoughts that it had all been *so wrong*.

But Lionel hoped—prayed in a way he hadn't since he was a boy—that Solomon had found some piece of peace.

Because Lionel knew he never would.

Not in this town.

Not in this life.

Not after what they'd done.

#

The morning after the real killer was announced, Beulah opened the store like she always did—door creaking wide at 7:00 sharp, blinds tied back, the bell overhead ringing, low and lonely. The air was thick with grief, shame, and regret.

117

The townsfolk came in pale, haunted, and heavy. They bought salt, flour, turpentine, and rumors. The real business of the day.

"I remember when she was found. Lying beside the tracks like a discarded rag doll."

"No clues. No evidence."

"They said that Moreau boy walked the tracks at night…"

"A lot of people said a lot of things…"

Beulah didn't repeat any of it. She didn't add to it. She just listened.

She knew how people lied to themselves when they needed a monster. And she remembered him—silent, strange, kind. The taffy jar. His quiet, unspoken thank you.

So, when the whispers grew into a bonfire of fear and men like Jules Rousseau started stomping around talking about *"taking care of things,"* she had said something few had the courage to say.

She said it in her store, to Jules' face.

"If you harm him without proof, you ain't justice. You're just a coward without any sense."

Jules didn't answer her. Just scowled, muttered something about "old women who don't know the world."

But the words stuck. Others heard. Some turned away. Not all. But some.

#

After the cabin and chase through the swamp, Beulah wore black—not for the child, not for Solomon, not just her. For what the town had let itself become.

And when the real killer was caught, it was Beulah who wrote a letter to the Baton Rouge newspaper and signed it with her full name. It was titled:

"We mourn two souls in Slidell. One was taken by evil. The other by our own fear."

It was never printed. But she kept a copy in the cash drawer. Right next to the jar of taffy.

For Solomon.

Just in case.

###

14. THE GROUND REMEMBERS

It started small.

The groundskeeper, old Mr. Fortier, noticed it first—a faint smell, sour and sharp, like iron and river rot. It lingered along the north fence, even when the wind blew clean.

Then came the disturbed earth.

Thirteen spots. Always thirteen.

Not dug up. Not trampled. Just... shifted, like something below had rolled over in its sleep. The dirt cracked and bulged, damp even on dry days. Once, he tried pressing it down with the heel of his boot—but the soil pushed back, soft and pulsing, like breath trapped under loam.

Then the animals stopped coming.

Birds no longer perched on the chapel spire. Stray dogs that used to curl up in the shade of tombs began to whimper and turn back at the gate. Once, a possum was found dead near the Duval crypt—jaw dislocated, eyes wide, body twisted as if it had fallen from a height. But there was no height nearby.

Children started talking about the woman in black.

They said she stood by the statue of Saint Margaret of Castello, late at night, motionless. Pale eyes, long hair that hung to the ground like vines. When spoken to, she vanished—not in a shimmer, but like fog dispersing. One boy said she wasn't a woman at all, but a shape that looked like one.

"She was listening," he told his mother. "She was waiting to hear the last piece."

That same week, symbols appeared on four gravestones.

Not carved—just smeared, in mud or ash. Circles broken by a single diagonal line. Always the same shape, always wiped clean by the next day, but always returning somewhere else. The priest said it was nothing. Just children. But even he stopped walking the grounds at dusk.

#

On Sunday morning, Rosalie passed by the cemetery gates and noticed thirteen black feathers laid in a row atop the stone wall. Each is slick with morning dew. None of them moved in the wind.

She stood there a long time, hand clutching the rosary at her breast, her lips parted in a prayer she never finished.

#

Some said it was a coincidence. Some said it was fear playing tricks.

But those who were there the night he died—the men who buried the pieces—they began to avoid the cemetery altogether.

Even in daylight.

Especially in daylight.

Because in the light, they could see the earth still heaving softly.

As if it remembered the thirteen sins and waited to raise them back up.

#

The Earth Stirs

It was just before dawn when Marie Moreau stepped onto the grounds of Saint Margaret's Cemetery.

She wore her dark shawl tight around her shoulders, the hem of her skirt trailing dew from the grass. No one saw her come. No one would admit to seeing her if they had.

She moved like a shadow through the graves, slow, deliberate, as though she felt each name, each stone. Her skin looked like weathered bark, and her eyes held something deeper than grief—knowing.

She passed the Virgin statue with no hands.

Paused.

Her fingers brushed the base of the stone. They lingered, as if they could pull meaning from silence.

Then she turned, as if led—not by sight, but by pull, by instinct, by something older than language.

She stopped at thirteen places. In no particular order. Never counting out loud. But at each spot, she knelt.

She touched the dirt.

She whispered—not in French, not in English, but in something older, something that crept like moss through the cracks of the world. Her words weren't loud. They weren't angry. They were gentle, like a mother trying to wake a sleeping child.

At the final mound—near the broken angel—she laid a single object.

An herb bundle wrapped in blue cloth, tied with red thread, the ends singed.

She placed it on the soil like a promise.

And then, as the sky began to shift into pale amber and the morning birds stirred, Marie stood, lifted her chin, and said aloud:

"You ain't alone, bébé. We ain't finished."

She turned without ceremony.

As she walked past the chapel, the stained-glass windows flickered, though the sun had not yet risen enough to strike them.

And far behind her, at the thirteenth grave, the herb bundle caught fire.

But it did not burn.

It glowed—blue at first, then gold, then vanished entirely into the ground.

#

Gervais hadn't slept more than a few hours a night since the night in the swamp.

He told himself it was his back. His lungs. The cough. But he knew better.

This night, sleep found him all at once. Deep. Hard. Final.

And then, the dream came—

He stood in the cemetery, barefoot, shirtless, a shovel in his hands. The moon overhead hung too low, too red. The graves were open—thirteen of them—not dug by man, but torn from the inside. And each one led downward, not into earth, but into rooms—cellars, basements, tunnels made of roots and bone.

He moved from one to the next.

In the first, he saw Solomon's hand, still twitching, clutching the burlap as if reaching out of the past. It pointed at Gervais.

The next showed a tongue writhing like a snake, whispering something Gervais could not understand—but he felt it. Shame. A hot, crawling shame.

In the third was a mirror, and when he looked in it, he saw himself buried under the hanging tree, eyes sewn shut, a burlap sack over his chest like a child's bib.

The ground shook.

And then came the voice, not Onionhead's, not Marie's—but something that lived between them:

"You scattered what you feared.

Now it knows where you live."

Gervais awoke in his bed, gasping, mud on his feet.

His hands were stained red.

Not blood, just red. Like rusted iron. Like old earth.

From that night on, he refused to walk past the cemetery. He stopped speaking at town meetings. He carved a small wooden crucifix from swamp cypress and carried it in his pocket everywhere—but it smelled of salt and sulfur, and left splinters no matter how smooth he polished it.

He did not speak of the dream. But his eyes changed.

He was no longer afraid of death.

He was more afraid of what might come before it.

#

By the second week after Onionhead's killing, the air in Slidell seemed to change.

The rain lingered longer than it should have, and the wind carried a strange sound—like weeping through the trees, but too steady, too rhythmic, as if it followed the streets themselves.

The people didn't talk about it, not directly. But the signs were there.

Miss Lucille Babineaux, the laundress, said her clotheslines had been pulled down in the night—knots untied, poles snapped clean in two. Her white linens had been dragged through the dirt and left in the shape of a man, arms outstretched, face toward the sky. She burned them. She didn't sleep the next night.

At the edge of town, Father Bellamy found the doors of Saint Margaret's Chapel wide open just before dawn. The altar cloth was soaked through—not with rainwater, but something dark and sticky. Beneath the crucifix, someone had etched a symbol into the stone with a blade or a nail: a broken circle, cut once through the middle.

The priest scrubbed it out, but it came back the next morning.

Then came the animals.

A mule collapsed on the road, twitching, foaming at its mouth. Dogs refused to bark near the cemetery. A cow gave birth to a still calf with no eyes, and her milk turned gray by the third day. The farmer poured it into the ditch, and the grass there has not grown back since.

Children whispered of a man made of sticks, standing in the woods near the Moreau trail. They said he didn't move, just watched. One child claimed it wasn't a man at all, but a bundle of pieces, walking on its own, "looking for the rest of itself."

Mothers pulled their children inside before the sun touched the trees. Windows were shuttered early. Church pews began to fill again, but no one sang.

Even the air smelled wrong.

Like bruised magnolia and rusting iron.

Mrs. Gautreaux, who once led the town's Easter play, said she woke up in the middle of the night to find her front door wide open. At her feet was a small object: a doll's head, scorched on one side, its eyes gouged out.

Still, no one mentioned Solomon's name.

But his absence hung in the air, heavier than his presence ever was.

And deep down, folks began to wonder:

Had they buried a man?

Or had they split something open that they couldn't put back together?

###

15. WHAT WON'T STAY BURIED

The meeting took place behind Dumont's Feed Store, in the half-rotted barn where dust hung like smoke and raccoons slept in the rafters. It was past midnight. No one knew they were there.

Gervais Boudreaux, Jules Rousseau, and Harlin Dupré sat in a triangle of flickering candlelight, surrounded by sacks of grain and the creak of unseen floorboards. A bottle of rye whiskey passed between them, but none of them drank much. Their hands trembled.

The only sound for a while was the drip of condensation and the occasional scratch of a rat in the walls.

Jules broke the silence. His voice was a rasp now, hollow from too much smoking and too little peace.

"You felt it, right?"

"This… pressure. Like something is watching."

Gervais gave a dismissive snort, but his eyes flicked sideways.

"It's the damn swamp playing tricks. Too much damp, too much wind. We're grown men. We don't go chasin' shadows like old widows with too many cats."

Harlin stared at the floor. His boots were caked in mud he hadn't been able to scrape off in days.

"Ain't the swamp," he said, voice low. "It's him. Or what's left of him."

The others stiffened.

Jules wiped sweat from his upper lip.

"Then why don't we say it? Out loud. What we did."

"We gave the town peace," Gervais said. "That's all. He was sick in the head. Not right. We did what the marshal didn't have the guts to do."

"We chopped him into thirteen goddamn pieces," Jules said. "Thirteen. That number doesn't sit right in the bones, Gervais. And you know it."

No one spoke for a long time. A thunder roll grumbled far off—no storm yet, but the suggestion of one. The air smelled faintly of burnt rosemary.

Harlin finally looked up. His eyes were bloodshot and wild.

"I saw him last night. In the cemetery. Or maybe it wasn't him, not whole. Just a shape. But it looked at me. And I couldn't move. Like I was held."

"Held by what?" Jules said, scoffing.

Harlin's face darkened.

"Held by regret. Or maybe revenge."

Jules stared at the candle, watching the flame bend like it was being breathed on from an unseen place.

"What if it wasn't just a man we killed?"

"Don't you start with that voodoo shit," Gervais snapped. "That's Marie's poison talk. Always was."

"You see her at the cemetery?" Jules asked. "She ain't mournin'. She's listening. Like she's waiting for an answer."

They all went quiet again. A rat skittered down the feed chute.

Then Harlin said, barely above a whisper:

"We didn't bury guilt. We planted it. And now it's coming up through the dirt."

The candle suddenly flickered sideways—without wind.

All three men jerked back.

"I'm leavin' town," Harlin said, standing too fast. "I don't care what you two do."

Gervais looked at him like he was insane.

"And what'll you tell folks?"

"Nothin'. I don't owe them a damn thing. But I ain't waitin' to be dragged into the ground piece by piece."

Jules didn't try to stop him.

He was listening—too hard now—to something outside the barn.

It almost sounded like footsteps on wet leaves.

###

16. VENGEANCE REPAID

Harlin Dupré

They found Harlin Dupré two days after he left town, holed up in a crumbling sugarcane shack just outside Bayou Dominque—or what was left of him.

The door was hanging open when the cane cutter boys found it. Flies buzzed thick in the air. The smell hit first—blood and rot, hot and damp like meat left out in the sun.

Inside, the shack was dark but not silent. The wind moaned through the cracks like something trying to speak.

Harlin's body was spread across the floorboards, but not whole.

His arms had been broken backward at the elbows and tied together with rusted wire behind his back. His mouth was sewn shut with fishing line. His eyes were gone—plucked clean—but no blood remained in the sockets, just two round hollows like dried clay bowls.

There were slashes up and down his torso—some ritualistic, some frenzied. The soles of his boots had been hammered through with nails.

But what stilled the room was the wall behind him.

Written in long, dripping streaks of his own blood was a signed message that read:

"IF YOU WERE THERE,

I'M COMING FOR YOU NEXT.

ONIONHEAD"

The letters were erratic, almost childlike in some spots, perfectly formed in others. Beneath the signature, the killer had left one final touch:

A single doll's eye, pressed into a knothole in the wood.

And beside it, resting like a relic, a withered herb bundle, tied with red thread.

#

The sheriff from Livingston called it an animal attack. Some said maybe Harlin went mad and did it himself. A few thought it could be someone from the cane fields who lost their temper. But no one believed any of it.

Word got back to Slidell by dusk.

By nightfall, Lyle Wesson's wife said she found him praying in the kitchen with a gun on the table and salt poured in a circle around his chair.

Gervais Boudreaux didn't come out of his house for three days.

And in the town square, carved into the bark of the old oak by the post office, someone had etched a name in shallow letters:

ONIONHEAD.

It hadn't been there the night before.

And no one claimed to have carved it.

#

After Harlin Dupré was found butchered in the cane shack, fear spread through Slidell like black mold in a closed-up room.

At first, folks whispered.

131

Then they locked their doors in broad daylight.

Church bells at the church and the cemetery chapel tolled off-beat, no one knowing who had rung them. The marshal drank more, but his face paled every time he passed the old cemetery. Even children—usually immune to grown-folk moods—stopped playing stickball and hopscotch. They spoke softly, glanced over their shoulders, and crossed themselves when they passed by trees with hollow trunks.

No one saw who did it.

But by the end of the second week, another man from the mob—Earl Staggs—was dead.

\#

Earl Staggs

They found Earl in his own home, hanging upside down from the rafters, throat slit so clean it looked surgical. But the blood hadn't pooled. It had been used.

It had been used to draw a map.

On the wooden floor beneath him, in crimson lines and curves, someone had painted a rough layout of the St. Margaret of Castello's Cemetery. Thirteen "X" marks dotted the map—each one corresponding, it would turn out, to a piece of Solomon Moreau's body. Earl's eyes had been torn out and nailed to the wall, as if watching what had happened to him.

And in the corner, once again, a signed message:

"IF YOU WERE THERE,

WHO WILL BE NEXT?

ONIONHEAD"

His tongue and teeth had been placed in a shallow bowl beside the map, wrapped in white muslin like a baptismal gift.

Outside, the town bell tolled nine times.

Though no one had pulled the rope.

#

Now the terror was open. People stopped going to work. Children were kept at home. The diner shut its doors. At St. Margaret's Chapel next to the cemetery, Father Bellamy burned incense nonstop and refused to speak Solomon's name, calling what was happening only *"the reckoning."*

Even strangers began to leave town. Drifters who had been sleeping near the train depot packed up and left without waiting for the train to arrive. One was found mumbling something about a man with *"a face like melted wax and a bag of bones on his back."*

They buried Earl Staggs in silence.

But on the day of the funeral, a stray dog dug up a small human finger bone near the plot.

#

The cicadas had gone quiet, and the moon hung low and yellow like an old bruise over Slidell.

Dr. Darryl Bergeron sat alone in his office, the oil lamp burning low, its wick cracked and stuttering. His ledger lay open on the desk before him—not for notes or names, but because he couldn't bring himself to close it. Not yet.

On page seventy-four, in his neat, looping script, was written:

133

"Mary-Ellen Ledoux. Five years old. Examination complete. Manner of death: blunt force trauma, manual strangulation, throat cut. Unnatural causes. Probable adult male assailant."

He had written it the very evening they brought her in. Before the whispering started. Before fear twisted into certainty and wrapped itself around that boy like a noose.

He had known.

Not with proof. Not with fire. But with a doctor's quiet instinct.

He'd known that what was done to that child had been done by someone older. Cruel. Measured. It didn't match Solomon's nature—or his capabilities.

But he hadn't spoken.

Because the truth wasn't louder than the town's grief.

Because guilt can be quiet.

And cowardice wears a clean shirt and a closed mouth.

He leaned back in the chair, eyes scanning the page. There, in the margin, he had once scribbled a note no one had seen:

"Strength mismatch. Carving not consistent with prior specimens. Consult Moreau?"

He had meant to speak with Marie Moreau. Ask her about the cedar dog. About Solomon's carvings. He remembered the way her eyes held storms. Maybe she would've said something then. Maybe she would've spit in his face. Either way, he hadn't gone.

He'd locked the drawer instead. Locked the words. Let the crowd speak in place of reason.

Now Solomon lay buried in the red earth behind the chapel, and the town walked a little slower, spoke a little softer, though no one ever said it plain.

That the wrong man had died—*an innocent man.*

That someone else had killed little Mary-Ellen. At first, he had thought it could be someone who may have watched as the mob marched into the swamp—or maybe even been part of it. Then news of the arrest had come.

Dr. Bergeron poured himself a small glass of rye. He didn't toast. He didn't mutter. He just sat with it in his hand like it was medicine that wouldn't work.

He thought of Solomon's hands—those trembling fingers working cedar and pine into soft, silent things.

And he whispered to the night: "I'm sorry, son."

#

Levon Coyle

Levon Coyle was known to carry a flask, even into church. They found him nailed inside his own smokehouse, slumped over the hooks like a carcass.

The floor was covered in blood and dead insects. His heart was torn out and nailed to a wall. The mouth had been sewn shut with swamp reeds—a bayou lily in each eye socket. His intestines were removed, laid around him in a circling pattern. His chest was split wide; ribs tied back with hemp cord. A bloody message was clearly written on the wall, in Levon's blood:

"IF YOU WERE THERE …

YOU'RE ALREADY DEAD.

ONIONHEAD"

A single porcelain doll was wedged in the door jamb, as if watching. The doll's porcelain face was broken—one side missing. The marshal took it, planning to compare it to the broken piece found in Mary-Ellen's grasping hand. He locked it away... the next morning, it was gone.

#

Burl Riggs, the Tracker

Burl Riggs had always been a dog man. His hound, Duke, was the finest tracker across three parishes. He'd trained the beast from a pup, fed him scraps from his own table, and slept beside him in the duck blind through more storms than he could count. And when the little girl went missing, it was Duke who led the search through the woods, nose to the ground, sniffing for a trail or clues.

Burl never thought twice about it. That was the dog's job.

#

Weeks after Onionhead's death, Burl began to notice changes in Duke.

The hound wouldn't sleep near him anymore. Wouldn't eat. Wouldn't meet his eyes. The once-loyal dog began growling low, ears flattened, hackles raised—as if Burl was a stranger.

One night, Burl woke to the sound of scratching. In the corner of the bedroom, Duke sat in the dark, staring at him, eyes glassy. Just watching. Hours passed before he finally moved.

Then the dog disappeared, ran away.

Three nights later, the neighbors saw smoke coming from Burl's barn.

When they arrived, they found what was left of Burl Riggs. The door had been barricaded shut from the inside, but there were no footprints in the dirt. No sign of struggle leading in or out.

Burl was nailed to the barn wall about a foot above the ground, spread wide like a crucifix. A rope was loosely tied around his neck, the rope he used as the dog's leash, the end looped over an old horseshoe nailed to the wall. His knees had been snapped backward. His mouth opened wide in a permanent scream, jaw broken. His eyes had been removed, one shoved into the bell of a hunting horn mounted beside his head, the other placed inside Duke's empty dog bowl, resting in a pool of blood.

His torso was opened—not slashed but 'unzipped' with inhuman precision from neck to groin. His guts were fed to Duke, whose blood-matted corpse lay curled beneath him. The hound died while chewing on something wet and pink—something of Burl's.

Written on the barn wall beside Burl was a message, written in thick, black smears of blood and bile:

"IF YOU WERE THERE AND BROUGHT THE HOUND,

NOW IT FEEDS ON YOU.

ONIONHEAD."

They say the barn never stopped stinking, even after the ashes cooled. And Duke? Some say his barking can still be heard echoing across the fields when the moon is thin and high.

But no dogs will go near that place now.

#

137

They met in the side room of Saint Jude's Church, beneath a worn crucifix and a wall lined with cracked jars of holy water. The town outside was silent—too silent—like it was holding its breath.

There were seven of them. Only three had taken part in the mob. The rest were those who felt the guilt of complicity. Those who'd cheered. Those who'd said nothing.

They sat in a ring of mismatched chairs, candles trembling on the wooden floor, sweat soaking through their clothes.

Reverend Landry stood at the head of the circle, his collar loose, his hands shaking. His Bible lay open but untouched.

"This town has blood on its hands," he said. "We let fear make us murderers. Now we must beg for forgiveness."

Mrs. Eloise Laroux, her hair wild and gray, spat on the floor.

"Forgiveness?" she snapped. "Forgiveness don't put bodies back together."

"No," said Tommy LaGrange, who'd bullied Solomon as a child. "But maybe it'll stop more from getting torn apart."

Silas Hayes, the undertaker's son, clutched a small sack of bones—fragments dug up from the cemetery. He set them gently at the center of the circle like an offering.

"I found these behind one of the mausoleums. They ain't nobody's we ever buried."

No one said anything.

The air grew thicker. One candle went out.

Then Ruth Fontaine, who had once slapped Solomon across the face when he asked for bread, spoke for the first time.

"What if we give the pieces back?"

The others turned.

"The pieces of him," she continued. "The ones that were scattered. What if we find them? Gather them up. Bring them to his grave. Or… wherever he is now."

Reverend Landry made the sign of the cross.

"A ritual," he said, half-whispering. "To put him to rest."

"A reburial," said Lionel. "All of him. Whole this time."

Eloise shivered.

"What if he don't want rest? What if he wants us?"

There was silence.

Then, slow and solemn, Silas opened a folded sheet of tattered parchment. A hand-drawn map—the same design painted in Earl Stagg's blood. Thirteen X's.

"We start here," he said, pointing.

"At the heart of the cemetery."

Unseen, from the church's rafters above, something stirred.

A spider spun a web across a crucifix.

A whisper passed through the walls—soft as mist, sharp as bone.

Outside, the church bell rang once.

No one had touched it.

And across town, the lights in Marie's window blinked out.

#

Marshal Kincaid hadn't slept in days.

139

The whiskey helped some, but the dreams were worse than the silence.

He sat in the chair by the window in his office—the only room in the whole jailhouse that still held heat—staring down the main street of Slidell like it owed him an answer.

The town looked wrong.

Trees hung too still. The gaslights burned a touch too blue. And the shadows didn't quite fall where they should.

Behind him, the holding cells were empty.

Had been since he locked up Solomon Moreau for "his own protection." That was before the fever took hold. Before the mob.

He hadn't stopped them.

He told himself it was because there was nothing he could do—not alone, not when the town's blood was up, not when grief turned to rage and rage to violence.

But that wasn't true.

The truth was, he'd been afraid.

Not of Solomon.

Of what he might represent.

A reckoning. A mistake too large to mend.

#

Now the men who'd tracked Onionhead through the swamp were dying in pieces. And the rest of the town was beginning to sense it, too—that some line had been crossed, and nothing would ever quite come back to the way it was.

Kincaid pulled the chain on the lamp.

Dim yellow light caught on the dust.

He looked down at the old photograph in his hand. A younger version of himself, arm slung over a teenage Solomon outside the Moreau cabin. He remembered that day. He'd brought flour and lard, and Marie had made tea with crushed mint and lemon balm.

Solomon had laughed once, softly, when the marshal told a joke about chickens.

He wasn't a monster then.

Hell, he never was.

#

The wind shifted outside. Not strong—but wrong.

It brought with it the scent of swamp water and burnt rope. Faint—but there.

He stood, holstered his pistol out of habit, and stepped outside.

That's when he saw it.

A doll. Sitting on the courthouse steps.

The same one he'd put in the evidence locker after Levon Coyle was killed. The one that had vanished during the night. It had a cracked porcelain face and wore a dress stained with mildew.

Pinned to its chest with a rusted nail was a scrap of paper.

Written in crooked, childish letters:

"YOU WATCHED.

YOU LET IT HAPPEN.

141

YOU'LL BURY YOURSELF NEXT."

The marshal staggered back.

His breath caught. His heart knocked against his ribs like it was trying to get out.

But he didn't cry out.

He didn't call for backup.

He just sat back in the chair by the window, the doll staring at him from the steps.

And he waited.

For morning.

For justice.

For Onionhead.

Whichever came first.

He was found the next day. The bullet had gone through the back of his throat, taking the bottom of his skull and spine with it. Only the marshal saw the doll. The note was pinned to his shirt. His death was ruled a suicide.

#

Frank Gautreaux

Frank, the old handyman who'd once shown Solomon kindness by offering food at his shed door, was found in his workshop—his death the cruelest irony.

The air inside the shop stank of blood and rotting wood. Tools hung perfectly in place, save for a small cleaver on the floor, slick with blood. Jessup's body was curled into the corner, as though trying to hide from something. His head was twisted

142

backwards, facing into the room, while his body faced the corner. His back had been broken—multiple times—until it curved almost back on itself. His chest cavity had been torn open with great force, and his heart removed—but it was found nearby, placed gently in a bowl of herbal tincture, as if preserved.

All around the body were dozens of tiny wooden dolls, their heads turned to face the corpse. Each doll had no eyes, just smooth, empty hollows. Frank's own eyes were replaced with small, polished river stones, slick and wet like they'd been taken from the swamp only moments before.

#

The townspeople begin to murmur about it: *"They all lost their eyes."*

Father Bellamy at St. Margaret of Castello's said that the wages of blind justice are blindness returned.

#

Now, even the most skeptical began to believe.

The town's older folks said Onionhead had been called back—by grief, by rage, or by something his mother did in the dark. Some whispered that Marie had traded her own spirit to bring her boy's back in pieces, to make the town feel every cut he'd suffered.

And somewhere in the woods, the old cabin stood.

Some swore they saw candlelight flickering inside.

A strange blue-white glow that seemed to move, at times.

#

143

Lionel Cormier

Lionel hadn't slept since that night in the swamp.

He told folks it was the heat, or the humidity, or the damn cicadas. But deep down, it wasn't any of those things. It was what he saw every night in the mirror. Not his face. Not exactly. Something behind it.

His reflection was watching him.

It started small. A flicker in the glass. A shadow where none should fall. He'd pause mid-shave, staring at his reflection, his familiar face... watching. Judging.

In the tavern, a few folks still talked of Onionhead in hushed whispers. They talked about the others—Harlan, Frank, Earl. All dead now. All gone in ways that made your spine twist.

Lionel hadn't *done* anything. He'd been there, yes. Lantern in hand. At the edge of the group. He remembered the pained and puzzled look on Onionhead's face. He remembered Marie's voice, rough and sharp, cutting through the trees like a curse:

"If you hurt my boy, you'll be cursed for life."

Lionel hadn't touched Solomon. He wanted to believe that mattered.

#

One morning, he found a small, smooth river stone sitting on his bathroom sink. Just one. Dull gray. About the size of an eyeball.

He threw it in the garden, telling himself it was nothing. But that night, it was back.

Now it sat on his pillow, cold as bone.

144

#

Lionel's reflection turned against him next.

First, they trembled—just slightly—as if breathing. Then, when he passed, they didn't follow correctly. His reflection lingered a second too long, lips moving when his were still. Eyes looking somewhere else—over his shoulder.

Twice, he smashed one.

But they always showed back up—whole and clean the next day.

He wondered if he was imagining things—hallucinating.

He'd ask the preacher. No... no, he couldn't do that. He'd be laughed out of town. Or worse, pitied. And pity rotted faster than guilt.

#

On the last day, Lionel locked every door and window, shuttered the house, and lit candles in every room. He covered each mirror with sheets, but still, he could feel their presence, like mouths waiting to speak.

At dusk, he uncovered just one. The large one in his parlor. The one he'd had since boyhood.

The sheet slid off. He stared.

In the mirror, he saw himself. He looked older, tired, lips twitching.

But over his left shoulder stood Onionhead.

Eyes hollow. Skin gray.

And then the reflection smiled.

#

They found Lionel Cormier the next morning, lying in the parlor. His face was a network of deep, jagged cuts, mirror shards still embedded, glittering like diamonds. His hands were shredded, as if he'd tried to claw his own face off. And—again—on the wall a message:

"IF YOU WERE THERE AND SAID NOTHING,

YOU ARE NOT INNOCENT.

ONIONHEAD"

He was pinned to the floor by a sliver of glass through the tongue, unable to scream; he had bled out slowly, surrounded by his own broken reflections, doing nothing.

His eyes were gone. Only perfectly circular mirrors remained, and even those seemed to stare back with accusation. His eyes were found on the mantle—staring into what was left of the mirror that hung there.

#

The morning after Lionel was buried, Father Bellamy found a porcelain doll resting on his grave, its one remaining eye looking up toward the sky. "Some dang kid's idea of a joke," he said to himself. But his hands were shaking as he picked up the doll. "You saw it, didn't you? And you didn't say a damned thing either."

He took the doll and carried it along the train tracks to the place where a small white cross had been placed. There was a gnarled and twisted wooden marker there, too. He placed the doll by the cross, said prayers over both, and walked away.

#

146

By this time, no one walked alone anymore. Fog settled heavier than ever, thick as stew, turning lanternlight into a dull glow. Doors were bolted after dark, windows boarded. In the tavern, whispers replaced laughter. Folks nursed drinks they didn't taste, eyes flicking toward the door with every creak.

"They say he's walking again," murmured Miss Ellie, the barkeep's sister, barely above a whisper. "Come back from the mud and moss, with no eyes but a thousand ways to see."

Someone laughed—too loudly—forced. No one joined in.

Outside, the wind blew through the willows with a sound like humming.

#

Lyle Wesson

They found Lyle face-down in the black water of the salt bog. He'd gone out with his dogs before dawn, but only the dogs came back—whimpering, soaked, and silent.

The search party spotted him at sundown, miles outside of town near Lake Pontchartrain. His arms stretched wide over the water, his back impaled by what looked like ancient cypress branches—thrust through muscle and bone like spit rods. His mouth was open in a silent scream, and a wreath of swamp moss had been shoved into his throat like stuffing.

His eyes were gone, sockets filled with salamander eggs, their jelly sacs glistening in the twilight. Someone whispered that they were starting to hatch. Inside his mouth: a single frog, still alive, nestled in his throat like a parasite. The nearby reeds were braided into a circle.

A trail of slick footprints led back into the swamp, but no one dared follow.

#

Maybell Allemond

Maybell had always been the kind of person who went along with the crowd. Never the first to act, never the one to shout the loudest. That was her way.

She hadn't touched Solomon the night of the killing. Just stood back in the orange firelight, trying not to look. But the smell of the swamp. The sounds Solomon made—it haunted her.

Afterward, she drank harder than usual. The guilt sat in her belly like spoiled meat, twisting.

#

Maybell first heard them at night.

Scratching beneath the floorboards.

The scratching didn't come from mice. It was bigger. Wet sounding. Almost human.

She froze in bed, listening. The old house sat on cypress stilts a few feet above the marsh line, and under it—where spiders nested and snakes curled for warmth—something moved.

She slid her shotgun from behind the door and crept barefoot across the warped floor. Every board groaned. She swore she could hear breathing beneath her, timed with her own steps, like something was tracking her from below.

There was no basement, no cellar in houses like hers. Just black mud, rot, and moonlit water under the slats.

She left the lantern burning that night.

The noise never stopped.

#

The next day, there was a knock that came from the floor. Not the front door. The floor.

Three slow taps. Then silence.

When she finally got the nerve to look outside, she found nothing but a small pile of graveyard dirt on the top porch step.

That day, she found a tiny wooden eye carved into the step. Rough, primitive. Just an oval with a pupil cut deep.

She gouged it out with a knife and burned it in the stove. That night, the scratching got louder.

#

She stopped going into town. Folks had started whispering about the deaths. Maybell wasn't a fool. She knew what was happening. She knew that Lionel had not touched Solomon either—but look how that turned out.

And the swamp was hungry.

Something down there moved now; she could hear it shifting during the day. She nailed the door shut, but every morning, the nails would be out again—stacked in a neat little pile on the kitchen table.

A single rat's eye was left in a teacup beside them.

Maybell wrote a letter to no one and left it on the kitchen table—where the nails had been stacked. It read: *"I didn't touch the boy. I didn't swing the axe. I just stood there. Please. That's got to mean something."*

#

The temporary town marshal found the house seemingly empty a few days later. The bedroom door had been nailed shut—from the inside.

Maybell was found nailed to the bedroom floor, barbed wire coiled tightly around her wrists and ankles, cutting into the bone. Her arms were spread wide, her legs pulled apart at grotesque angles.

Rats had eaten her alive, starting at the feet. There was nothing below the knees but chewed stumps, tendons still twitching when they touched her.

Her stomach was hollowed out, her ribs cracked open, her lungs pulled through the gap and chewed to ribbons.

And the eyes?

Gone.

But not missing.

They were nailed to the ceiling, directly above her—so that if she had looked up in her final moments, she'd be staring back at herself.

The only sound in the room was the slow, rhythmic scurrying of rats. But the floorboards, some say, echoed with faint footsteps long after the body was removed.

And this time, on the wall, the message said:

"IF YOU WERE THERE AND SAID NOTHING

YOUR SILENCE WAS BITING.

ONIONHEAD"

\#

Children began refusing to sleep alone. One girl, Betsy Claire, was found outside at dawn, curled in the dirt, whispering to a porcelain doll with one missing eye. "She keeps me safe," she said, rocking gently. "She says the one with no face is near."

The townsfolk dismissed it as childish fear—until the doll began appearing in places it shouldn't have. Perched atop fences. Left inside the church. Set gently on windowsills.

Always facing inward.

And every time it appeared, something happened… as if the doll was there to witness.

#

Billy Simms

The St. Margaret of Castello Chapel's bell hadn't rung in days, not since Father Bellamy stopped services. But on the fourth night after Maybell's death, the bell began to toll by itself just before dawn.

A small gathering of townsfolk crept through the fog to the chapel. What they found would fracture their faith. Billy Simms, former deacon, hung crucified inside the belfry, body splayed across the old timber beams. Railroad spikes pierced his wrists and ankles, blood looking like rust, already spreading from the wounds. His flesh had been meticulously peeled and nailed to timbers. His ribs had been pried open, each broken and curled back like insect legs, exposing the dark cavity of his chest. His genitals were found in a mason jar filled with black swamp water.

Billy's eyelids were sewn shut; black thread crisscrossed like stitches on a doll. When the coroner unpicked them later, his sockets were filled with cold ashes, as though the eyes had burned to ash inside his skull. No message appeared on any of the walls—but it was found later, carved into the bones of the ribcage:

"IF YOU WERE THERE,

THE BLOOD SINGS YOUR NAME.

ONIONHEAD"

They found Billy's horse tied up outside the chapel. The horse was skittish and nervous. Freshly branded on its flank was a circle with a slash.

\#

A week after the bell tower crucifixion, the chapel was set ablaze in the dead of night. No one claimed to see who did it. No one admitted to hearing the roar of the fire. No one saw the flames leaping skyward. But the next morning, the steeple lay in blackened ruin.

At the edge of the ash pile, someone had placed two river stones—side by side, like eyes. Father Bellamy stood before the smoldering wreck, clutching his Bible like a shield.

"This town sinned in silence," he said, voice trembling. "And now the silence comes to collect."

No one dared speak. Behind them, the burned bell clanged once, all on its own.

\#

The porch outside the feed store sat slanted in the heat, warped boards creaking beneath boots gone still.

Gervais stared into his coffee like it held answers. It didn't. His face, once flushed with rage and certainty, was gaunt now—sunken at the cheeks—jaw clenched so tight his molars ached.

Jules sat beside him, massive hands folded in his lap. They were scarred from work, and from other things too—things he'd stopped justifying weeks ago.

The town around them had grown quiet. Dogs wouldn't bark. Birds didn't sing. Windows stayed shut even in the sweltering heat.

#

Nine of them were dead.

Not all at once.

But steady. One by one.

Slaughtered in ways no preacher dared name from the pulpit.

Only the two of them remained.

"Y'ever think maybe we went too far?" Jules said, voice low, like the words themselves might summon something.

Gervais didn't answer. He hadn't slept. Not really. Not since the night he'd seen the reflection of something standing behind him in the cracked bathroom mirror—something tall and wrong, with no eyes. When he turned, the room was empty.

"Don't start that," Gervais muttered. "He was a freak. Everyone knew it. That girl—"

He stopped short.

They both knew that Onionhead hadn't touched that girl. That he was innocent.

They knew it now.

Jules shifted in his chair, eyes darting across the empty street. A curtain twitched in a window. A sign clattered against the post office door. Dust curled in the gutter like cigarette smoke.

153

"You hear somethin'?" Luke asked.

"No."

But Gervais didn't sound sure.

From behind the feed store, something knocked once, like wood against wood.

Then again.

Then three times faster.

Neither man stood.

They just sat in the slow-cooking silence, like two ghosts in waiting, each wondering who would go first... or if something worse was coming for the last two.

#

Jules Rousseau

Jules had nightmares about the railroad tracks. That's where they'd found the girl. That's where he kept seeing her face.

He was discovered one dawn lying across the rails. His hands had been torn from his wrists—not cut, not severed—ripped away. They were nowhere to be found. Only his torso remained intact—his lower body crushed, guts sprayed in a fan pattern across the gravel, his spine dangling like a wet rope.

The strange part? No train had passed that night.

His eye sockets were plugged with gravel, packed so tight they cracked the surrounding bone. A tiny wooden crow figurine sat on his chest, soaked in blood.

Carved into what was left of his chest was the message:

"IF YOU WERE THERE AND RAISED YOUR FISTS,

YOUR HANDS BELONG TO ME.

ONIONHEAD."

…and then there was one.

#

The church bells rang on Sunday, but the pews were half-empty.

Those who came sat in clusters, not families. No one sang the hymns. No one dared glance toward the back row—where the widows sat weeping and a young man near the aisle refused to remove his hat. His hands trembled too much.

The preacher's voice cracked halfway through Psalm 94:

"He that chastiseth the heathen, shall not he correct?"

"He that teacheth man knowledge, shall not he know?"

A baby cried. A man stood up and walked out.

Outside, the summer heat hung thick, but it didn't feel like summer anymore. Shops kept their signs turned to "Closed." Doors stayed bolted, even in the daylight. Windows were curtained with bed sheets and old quilts, anything that made it harder to see in or out.

Children weren't allowed to play near the woods or the tracks. They stayed close to home and whispered in corners, saying names they weren't supposed to know.

Solomon. Onionhead. Willy-the-Wisp.

At the general store, a man named Clay Benton dropped a sack of flour when a shadow passed the window. He cursed, but

155

quietly. He had been friends with Gervais—once. He hadn't gone with him that night, but he knew. Knew too much.

"I didn't throw a punch," he'd told his wife.

"But you didn't stop them either," she'd whispered back, eyes wide, voice thin.

She slept with the Bible beneath her pillow now. And a kitchen knife.

Down near the mill, two women swore they saw something tall standing by the willows. Said, it didn't move. Said, it had no eyes. Said, it just watched.

The acting marshal didn't respond to calls after dark anymore. The doctor drank now, when he thought no one saw him. The preacher stopped walking past the burned-out chapel.

The town was unraveling.

Not just from grief.

Not just from guilt.

From the silence came the creeping certainty that no one was safe, because someone—or something—knew.

#

Gervais Boudreaux

Gervais Boudreaux had been a father once.

His little girl, Lettie, had his eyes. Her laughter used to fill the whole of their lean, shotgun-style house on the edge of town.

Lettie had gotten very ill one winter. The doctor did what he could, but it wasn't enough. Gervais refused to head into the swamp for help, and when a packet of herbs appeared at his door, he threw them in with the rest of the garbage. A few days later, another bundle appeared. It, too, was tossed away.

That's why the silence now was worse than anything. Worse than the others' deaths. Worse than what they'd done to that boy out in the swamp.

He still remembered it. Onionhead lying curled up on muddy ground, face barely human in the torchlight, those huge, misshapen eyes filled not with rage but with something worse: understanding.

Like he knew how this would end, even then.

Like he pitied them.

#

Now Gervais sat alone in his locked parlor, three shotguns, a belt of shells, a Bible he hadn't touched in years, and a bottle of rye that never left his hand.

The lamps were all lit.

The windows were covered.

The air was too still.

He hadn't slept in days. Sleep brought the dreams—visions of Mary-Ellen standing at the foot of his bed, her doll clutched to her chest with its broken half-face.

And behind her, always, the tall shadow.

Solomon.

Or what was left of him.

No, not Solomon—Onionhead!

He heard the nickname echo in his skull like a curse.

157

#

The scratching started around midnight.

Not at the door, not at the windows.

Under the floor.

Slow. Patient. Like long fingernails on dry wood. Gervais froze. His breath caught in his throat. Then a whisper.

"Thirteen."

He fired the first barrel into the floor. Splinters flew. Nothing there.

The second shot cracked through the pantry.

Nothing.

Then silence.

He stood, trembling, just a man again, no longer a grieving father, no longer a righteous voice.

Just a coward in a dying house.

#

Then the doll appeared—right where Lettie used to sit. On the rocking chair.

It wasn't there before—but there it was now. Watching.

He hadn't put it there.

He wouldn't have.

It rocked once.

Twice.

Stopped.

He thought he heard a voice, as soft as smoke and as cold as bone:

"You were first. So, you will be last."

The lights went out.

Something wet and ancient slipped behind his eyes.

And Gervais finally screamed.

#

They never found his body.

Only thirteen teeth were arranged in a circle around his empty boots in the middle of the floor. And scratched into the floorboards, in shaky childlike scrawl:

"He was there; worse than them all.

Now he is gone. Where?—I won't say.

Now I can rest. Remember me."

#

Sometimes, at night, folks claim to see two dim lights floating in the darkness. At times in the St. Margaret Cemetery. Other times, near the white cross and the twisted marker beside the tracks. And sometimes, headed to or coming through the trail that leads to the Moreau cabin.

The killings stopped after Gervais's death. But the swamp seemed to grow darker, thicker, angrier. No one walks the Moreau trail anymore.

###

17. WHAT LINGERS

In Slidell, the camellia bushes and wisteria bloomed all at once, climbing up porch columns and curling like smoke around iron gates. The cane fields grew tall and green again, and the cypress trees stopped weeping for a while.

The deaths had stopped, too.

No more bloody walls, no more missing livestock, no more dolls appearing randomly in odd places. The graveyard, once restless, now sat quiet beneath a soft quilt of moss and moonlight.

People walked slower. Spoke less. Looked over their shoulders more.

No one ever talked about Solomon Moreau—not directly. They called it "the trouble," if they mentioned it at all. But children who wandered too far into the swamp were still pulled back quickly. Doors were bolted before sundown. And sometimes, in the low light before dawn, someone might whisper:

"Best not dig up the past in Slidell. It tends to dig back."

#

The old chapel bell never rang again.

Reverend Landry held services with Father Bellamy, but fewer people came. There was talk of a new marshal, but nobody wanted the job. Gervais Boudreaux was never seen again after that night. A few say he went north. Others say he never left. No one really bothered to look.

One child claimed to have seen Gervais walking through the graveyard, head bowed, a doll tucked under one arm.

No one asked questions.

160

#

Slidell is quiet now.

But it is a haunted quiet.

The kind that settles in the bones.

The kind born not of ghosts, but of fear left to rot, of innocence crushed underfoot, and of what happens when a town chooses fear over mercy.

Solomon "Onionhead" Moreau is gone.

But the wound he left behind never fully closed.

And sometimes—just sometimes—the swamp seems to hum his name.

###

18. THE PERPETUAL GUARDIAN

Many say he's there now.

Out past the weeping cypress trees and the rusted gates, where the Spanish moss hangs like funeral veils and the ground stays soft no matter the season—"Onionhead", laid to rest (or what they could find of him) beneath an odd-shaped stone on the outer edge of St. Margaret's Cemetery. Father Bellamy spoke— in the hope that it would bring peace to his soul.

It wasn't consecrated ground where they put him. They didn't dare dig deep. Some say they buried him face down, or with salt in his mouth. Superstition's a funny thing. Especially when it feels earned.

But now folks talk in whispers about how the cemetery changed after he was buried.

No one saw the burial. Not really. The constable claimed he was "handled proper." But no one saw the box go into the ground. No one saw the body.

And now...

Now there is talk.

Caretakers won't stay past dusk. Groundskeepers won't go alone. One boy dared his friend to knock three times on Onionhead's stone, and the friend hasn't spoken since. He just stares at the walls and cries without knowing why.

Some say if you visit the cemetery after sundown, the gate won't open again until morning, as if the iron itself doesn't want to let go. Others speak of hearing footsteps, slow and wet, crunching gravel that never leaves a trail.

A gravedigger, called Old Marty, swears he saw something just after the last storm—moving between the headstones without sound.

He said it wasn't looking for anything.

Just watching. Guarding.

"Do not disturb the rest of its citizens," he mumbles now, always, mostly to himself.

"Do not call him up. Do not speak too loud."

"St. Margaret's got a new guardian, and he ain't at peace."

#

The children call him **The Hollow Man**, or **The Quiet Watcher**—not wanting to say his real name out loud.

Sometimes they leave flowers on his grave. Sometimes they leave 'eyes'—marbles, doll's eyes, bits of glass—without knowing why.

And in the town, folks cross themselves when thunder rolls from the south.

Because Onionhead may be dead... but his spirit's awake. And the souls of St. Margaret of Castello Cemetery rest easy only so long as he stays watching.

###

A few years later, when Maman Marie passed, the swamp wept with rain for three days. Her body was delivered to the doctor's office. The next day, it was gone, vanished like morning fog in the rising Sun. It was never found, but the crumbling cabin

163

remained. Some desperate people still visit it sometimes, when the air is thick with need—and if they listen closely, they swear they hear her whispering through the trees:

"Not all medicine is made for the body. Some is meant for the soul."

#

And deep in the swamp, where the mist never lifts and the trees grow too close, there still stands the ruin of a cabin, vines grow over the collapsing foundation like veins on an old hand.

Sometimes, when the moon is full, folks swear they hear footsteps in the water. Not heavy. Soft. Barefoot. Like someone walking home in the dark, unafraid.

#

Rosalie Thibodeaux, now older, tends to the little herb garden Marie had once kept. She left small bundles of rosemary and rue at the edge of the woods—just in case. She claimed it was for the raccoons, but folks knew better.

Some say Rosalie still heard Solomon's voice on the wind, humming half-remembered lullabies.

Some say she never stopped mourning him.

###

19. THE LEGACY

The Lantern in the Cypress, c.1960

Deep in the heart of the swamp, South of Slidell, Louisiana, where the cypress trees lean like old men with secrets and the moss hangs heavy like ghosts in the night, there once stood a weather-worn cabin. It wasn't on any map, and no road led to it, only a narrow waterway known to locals and forgotten by time. A path once led from the railroad tracks to the cabin, but hurricanes and storms had washed out the trail long, long ago. Folks around Slidell whispered about the cabin, especially after too many drinks or when the fog rolled in thick. Some said it was cursed. Others said it was just old. Many said it was just legend and superstition, stories born from imagination and fear. But all agreed on one thing: you didn't go near it after sundown.

#

Cecile Broussard didn't believe in ghost stories.

She was a wildlife photographer and had come to the swamp chasing rumors of an ivory-billed woodpecker—believed extinct but occasionally sighted by those inclined to exaggeration. She rented a pirogue—a small Cajun flat boat—from a grizzled man named Jojo who squinted when she mentioned the area near Devil's Bend. He warned her: "If you see a light hangin' over the water that ain't got no source, turn back. Don't follow it."

Cecile smiled politely and paddled off before sunrise, camera slung over her shoulder.

The swamp was alive. Dragonflies skimmed the surface of still water. Egrets rose like feathered ghosts into the pink morning sky. She saw no rare woodpecker, but she did find

165

something else—a glint through the trees, faint and yellow. A window?

Curiosity pulled harder than fear. She followed a narrow break in the reeds until a cabin revealed itself, shrouded in moss and time. It sat on stilts, barely above the water, wooden slats warped by age and humidity. A rusted lantern swung gently on the porch beam. The light inside flickered. Someone was there.

"Hello?" she called. No answer.

She tied her skiff to a post and stepped onto the porch. The door creaked open with a reluctant sigh. Inside, it was cool and shadowed. Dust floated in the sunlight like ash. The furniture was old, but not abandoned. A rocking chair sat mid-motion, as if someone had just left it. On the table was a photograph—black and white, curled at the edges, very old. A man in overalls, a woman in a white dress, both smiling with solemn eyes. Behind them, the same cabin, only newer, brighter.

Then came the sound—a slow drip, like water from a faucet. But it came from the far room, the one with the closed door. She stepped closer. The air grew colder.

Drip.

She opened the door.

It was a bedroom or had been. The bed was made, covered in a quilt of faded blues and reds. In the corner stood a basin of water, and above it hung another photograph—this one of a girl, maybe five or six, holding a carved wooden bird with outstretched wings.

Suddenly, the lantern outside swung hard, clanging against the beam. The wind howled through the broken shutters, though no storm brewed. Cecile turned sharply and saw her. A figure in the hallway mirror. The girl from the photograph, pale and wet, her eyes hollow as old oyster shells. Behind her stood a dark figure, without features—like a watchful shadow. Startled, she turned to see that the room was empty.

Cecile stumbled back, knocking over the basin. Water splashed across the floor. She didn't stop to gather her gear. She fled, heart hammering, down the porch, into the skiff, and didn't look back until the cabin was hidden again behind the trees.

She never found the ivory-billed woodpecker. But when she developed her film weeks later, one photograph stopped her cold.

It was of the cabin, taken from her skiff, in the early morning light.

In the window, a face.

Young. Wet. Smiling.

The locals still talk about her— "that girl from the city" — and how she came out of the swamp wide-eyed and shaking. But the cabin?

It's still there.

And some nights, if you're near Devil's Bend, you may see a lantern swinging through the cypress.

Best keep paddling.

#

The Dare, c.1985

The old cemetery gate creaked the same way it always had.

Even after the town installed the new iron fence in '72 and trimmed back the climbing moss every spring, the gate still groaned like it remembered. Remembered the night thirteen small graves opened when no one was watching. Remembered what the ground was forced to swallow.

Four teenagers stood just outside the gate, flashlights off, hearts pounding. It was Friday night, and the air was thick with insects and moist heat.

"You gotta go in alone," said Travis Boudreaux, the biggest of the boys, voice full of bravado he didn't really feel. "All the way to the back. Past the thirteenth marker."

"And leave the onion," added Celine Daigle, smirking. "Or he won't let you back out."

They all laughed—too loud, too sharp. Nervous laughter, the kind that comes when you're close to something old and wrong.

The youngest, Daniel, held the small white onion in his hand like it was a crucifix. It had been his turn, and he'd agreed to the dare, even if his stomach twisted every time he thought of the old stories his Tante Althea whispered when she drank too much coffee:

"Mind yourself, cher. Be good. 'Cause if you lie, or steal, or sass your mama -Onionhead'll find you. He don't need eyes to see."

The cemetery smelled like mildew and rusted time.

Daniel crept between crooked stones, past cracked angels, past the marble statue missing its head. His flashlight jittered in his hand as he counted:

One grave.

Two.

Three…

He didn't want to keep going, but the pull was real—not peer pressure anymore, something else. Like the land wanted him deeper in.

By the time he reached the thirteenth marker, the air felt different.

Too still.

Too cold.

The ground was damp, though it hadn't rained in days. And there, nestled beneath a crooked stone cross with no name, was a small pile of teeth.

Daniel gasped.

He dropped the onion.

And the wind whispered:

"Good boy."

#

Most houses have television antennas. Kids wear Walkmans.

But in Slidell—

No one dares walk through the cemetery after dark.

Children are taught not to speak his name indoors.

And every Halloween, parents still carve onions into strange shapes, hollowed like turnips, and set them on porches—not for fun, but for protection.

Teachers at local elementary schools are forbidden from telling the story. But kids whisper it anyway, wide-eyed, gathered around lunch tables and fire pits:

"They chopped him up."

169

"Thirteen pieces."

"Buried him everywhere, and nowhere."

"But his mama, that swamp witch, she never gave up. And the swamp never forgets."

And when a child lies, or steals, or acts cruel, their parents don't need to raise a hand.

They just say softly:

"Onionhead's watching."

And the child goes still, eyes wide, as though they've heard something rustling just outside the window.

---

20. THE LEGEND CONTINUES

Slidell may seem quiet now.

Babies are born, crops are planted, bells toll for the dead and the wed alike. The swamp keeps her secrets just beneath her still skin, and most folks go about their days without thinking of the boy with the crooked head and the quiet eyes.

But the land remembers.

And the dead?

They don't sleep easy here.

For what was done in rage, what was buried out of fear, was never truly laid to rest.

They chopped him into thirteen pieces not to destroy him, but to scatter the truth, to keep it from ever rising whole. But in doing so, they cursed the land—cursed themselves. Because vengeance, once summoned and denied its justice, becomes something colder. Smarter. Patient.

And the truth?

The truth does not rot.

It waits.

It settles into the soil.

It grows back in whispers and weeds, in children's stories, in sleepless nights and unfinished prayers.

So, if you find yourself walking the old paths near the swamp, and the moon is thin, and the wind feels like breath against your neck, do not speak his name.

Not even in jest.

171

Because somewhere beyond the thirteenth grave, or the rubble where the cabin once stood, or in the hollow trunk of a moss-choked cypress, a piece of him still listens.

Still watches.

Still waits.

And if Slidell ever forgets what it did—if it grows cruel again, blind with fear or anger—he will rise again.

And this time,

he won't come alone.

END

Field Notes – SLIDELL MUSEUM ARCHIVE LOG, ENTRY #238

Recorded by G.D. Scott, Town Historian | June 3, 2020

I wasn't looking for ghosts.

I was sorting through decaying records in the archive storeroom—mostly mold-stained school registers and Confederate pension files—when I found a dusty envelope marked only with the initials S.M. Inside, wrapped in wax paper and bound with fraying twine, was a single page titled *"Witness to the Reckoning."*

The language was dated, the tone melodramatic by modern standards, but something about it lingered. Something old. Heavy.

I ran cross-reference research on the name Solomon Moreau. Nothing in official death records. No official grave marker noted. No census listing after 1925. Local newspapers from the time refer obliquely to *"a series of tragedies," "unrest in the town,"* and *"mob interference in ongoing investigations."*

But no names. No charges. No resolution.

Strangely, I've begun to notice how many people in Slidell still recognize the name "Onionhead"—though they rarely say it outright and only know it by reputation and rumor. Children sometimes whisper it on the playground. Teenagers dare each other to walk through the cemetery at night. Adults know him from the stories of their parents and grandparents.

I can't confirm if Solomon Moreau ever truly existed. But something did. Something that left a mark deep enough to fester under the skin of the town for nearly a century.

But for the record—for myself—I'll write this plainly:

If we're still telling the story, the memory still lives.

And if it still lives in our memories,

maybe it's not done with us yet.

— *G.D.S.*

"THE LEGEND OF ONIONHEAD"

as published and presented in tours by the Slidell Museum, Slidell, Louisiana.

[This version has been compiled from sources on file in the Slidell Museum.]

by Gregory Scott, 2020

- Folklore -

The legend of Onionhead dates to the early part of the 1900s, when Slidell was still just a very small town. Outside the town limits, there was a cabin in the wooded swamp. Legend says that this cabin was home to a giant of a man, a 'gentle-giant'—kind, gentle, easy-going—with a grotesquely disfigured face who lived there with his aging mother. This man would roam the woods but avoided coming into town, where the townsfolk had cruelly nicknamed him "Onionhead."

Some stories say he was born with a birth defect. Other stories claim that it was the result of an early childhood disease. Whatever the cause, he grew up from an early age with a distorted head and grotesque face. Onionhead stayed in the woods with his mother, hardly ever venturing into town and subjecting himself to the taunts and jeers of the people.

One day, a 5-year-old girl went missing in town. The girl's body was discovered the next day. She had been brutally murdered along the railroad tracks. People were outraged and eager for justice. Some of the townsfolk decided that the killer must have been the disfigured man living in the swamp. Before the town's marshal and authorities had a chance to investigate, a

175

mob formed. A group of angry citizens headed into the wooded swamp to confront Onionhead at his cabin. Onionhead heard the shouting and saw the angry crowd approaching. Fearing the mob, he fled into the swamp.

His mother stepped out of the cabin onto the front porch to try to calm the rowdy mob. Onionhead's mother was a '*traiteur*,' a Louisiana medicine woman who used sacred practices, medicinal herbs, and healing rituals to help people in need. (Some versions claim she was a voodoo witch.) The members of the mob did not want to listen to reason. They were itching for her son's blood. She threatened the angry crowd, saying that a curse would befall anyone who harmed her "baby boy."

They ignored her warnings and headed into the swamp to hunt Onionhead down. They eventually tracked him to a ditch where he was hiding. Filled with rage, seeking revenge and justice, the mob brutally killed him and dismembered his body. They cut the corpse into thirteen pieces and buried the parts throughout a local cemetery.

A few days later, the town's marshal located and captured the girl's real murderer. The killer had been a drifter passing through town. Members of the mob quickly realized that the gentle giant of a man, whom they had cruelly nicknamed Onionhead, was innocent and had been killed unjustly.

Not long afterward, there was a series of gruesome murders around town. The murdered people were found brutally killed in grisly ways. All the victims had one thing in common… every one of them had been part of the mob that murdered Onionhead. At every one of the crime scenes, the killer had left a message on the wall, written with the victim's blood.

The message simply said, "If you were there, I am coming for you next," and was signed, "Onionhead."

The legend says that once all the members of the mob had died, the spirit of Onionhead settled into the graveyard. People say that Onionhead is now the perpetual caretaker of that graveyard and waits for anyone who is foolish enough to enter the cemetery late at night.